Race for the Roses

Race for the Roses

LAURAINE SNELLING

Published by eChristian, Inc.
Escondido, California

Mission  **Books**

Race for the Roses

© Copyright 2012 by Lauraine Snelling. All right reserved.

Previously published by Heartsong Presents Book Club,
a division of Barbour Publishing, 1999, under ISBN: 1-57748-635-8.
©1999 by Barbour Publishing, Inc.

First printing in 2012 by eChristian, Inc.
eChristian, Inc.
2235 Enterprise Street, Suite 140
Escondido, CA 92029
http://echristian.com

ISBN: 978-1-61843-158-5

Published in association with the Books & Such Literary Agency, 52 Mission Circle, Suite
122, PMB 170, Santa Rosa, CA 95409-5370, www.booksandsuch.com.

Cover and interior design by Larry Taylor.
Cover photo: ©Cheryl Quigley /Dreamstime.com

Produced with the assistance of The Livingstone Corporation. Project staff includes: Dan
Balow, Afton Rorvik, Linda Taylor, Sharon Wright, Ashley Taylor, Lois Jackson, and Tom
Shumaker.

Printed in the United States of America

19 18 17 16 15 14 13 12 8 7 6 5 4 3 2 1

Mission Books

Prologue

I'm sorry, Son, but I have to leave now."

"But Daddy." Seven-year-old Dane Morgan looked up at his father, tears swimming in blue eyes that matched his father's. "I don't want you to go."

"I know, Son, neither do I." Hubert Morgan ignored the creasing of his dress khakis as he knelt and gathered his son into his arms. "But I have to." He tipped his son's face up with one caring finger under the quivering chin. "You must be the man of our house until I come home again; do you understand?"

The boy shook his head and tried to bury his face in his father's shoulder.

Hubert kept a firm hold on his son's chin. "That means you must take care of your mother and sister, keep them safe until I return."

"I . . . I w–will, Daddy." The small boy straightened and touched two fingers to his forehead in the salute his father had taught him. "Yes, sir." His chin quivered again. One tear trickled over the curve of his round cheek. "I will t–take care of Mama and Sissy." He snapped his arm back to his side.

Hubert Morgan stood and returned the salute. "Bye, Son. See you in a few months. I'll be praying for you every day."

"Me, too. Bye, Daddy," the boy whispered as his father, shoulders and back straight as the Marine Corps demanded, walked toward the waiting plane. While Dane felt his mother's hand on his shoulder, he never took his eyes off the plane until he could see it no longer.

ONE

Thirty Years Later

Wispy veils of ground fog hovered over the oval track and white-fenced infield of Portland Meadows Racetrack. As Robynn O'Dell trotted the bay Thoroughbred onto the sandy course, the horses galloping in front of the grandstand appeared legless, phantom creatures floating on a drifting sea.

"Easy, fella," she crooned, her musical voice a counterpoint to the grunts of the straining horse. "You can let it out later." Robynn gentled him with her voice, rising in the short stirrups to gain greater control.

With the sensitive hands and perfect balance of a born horsewoman, she kept the seventeen-hand colt at the easy lope she knew would build the greatest endurance. As her mount settled down to serious work, Robynn glanced at the overcast sky.

"Do not rain," she ordered the scurrying clouds. *Heavenly Father, we need a good fast track, not ankle-deep mud. I'm tired of washing half of Oregon down the drain after every race.* While she knew the prayer was only a holdover from early days, still it didn't hurt to invoke the name of the Almighty, in case He might be listening—not that she was convinced He cared about such a mundane request.

As if on cue, a silver disk of pale sun appeared low in the east, floating behind thin clouds. A few strides later, the cloud bank blotted it out again.

When Robynn and her mount swept by the entry gate, she felt a tingling up her spine. The desire to turn and see who was watching her almost broke her concentration on the animal she rode so effortlessly. After several more circuits of the track, she pulled the steaming horse down to a sidestepping trot.

Robynn switched her one-piece rein to her left hand so she could push up her goggles and wipe her dripping eyes on her other sleeve. October mornings in the Pacific Northwest had a real bite to them. In all her twenty-five years of living there, she hadn't adjusted to it.

Steam billowed from the tired horse as she slowed him to a walk just before they exited for the stables.

The tingling sensation rippled up her back again. Startled, Robynn searched every face until her violet eyes locked with the electric blue gaze of a tall, broad-shouldered man in a sheepskin jacket. He leaned against the fence as if he owned it. Her breathing quickened as the moment stretched to include the sun breaking through just in time to set the fog droplets sparkling in his blue-black hair. The tingle spread to her middle, then up to her face. She could feel the heat warring with her chilled skin.

As her horse sidestepped through the gate, Robynn could still feel the man's gaze on her back. The desire to turn and look at him again ate at her mind, singing out to her fingers. She clenched her hands on the reins, willing them and herself to behave. Why, she'd never even seen the guy before, let alone met him. Who was he? He acted as if he owned not only the track but the entire world. He'd stared at her and her horse as though they were on display just for him.

Who was she? Dane Morgan couldn't keep his gaze off her. The petite woman rode with the effortless skill of a natural rider, but that wasn't the only thing that drew his attention. He could barely see her face, hidden by the goggles and racing helmet, so it wasn't that.

Maybe it was the control he sensed. Control and power were entities he'd understood. He'd used both in building Morgan, Inc., to its present level of success. While he fully credited his employees with implementing the team-management principles long before the concept became a buzz word, he knew the personal power it took to make everything come together. Plus the time. And the effort.

Which was why he'd finally taken some time to indulge in his hobby, Thoroughbred horse racing. He came by the love of horses naturally, his grandfather bred them, his uncle Josh trained them, and his mother had been a steeplechase jockey—before the accident. Now she only jockeyed her wheelchair.

His gaze kept returning to the woman slow galloping her feisty mount around the track. *Wouldn't you know?* He shook his head. *She rides Thoroughbreds.* Well, he'd make sure he met her before he left, to get rid of the attraction if nothing else. Just like all the other attractive women he'd met, once she opened her mouth, he'd lose interest. Maybe his mother was right: No flesh and blood woman could ever measure up to his fantasy of perfection.

He shook his head. He was here to look for horses, and he hadn't even noticed the mount she rode. Maybe he was just tired. Or lonely. Or both.

"You and Dandy looked real good out there, Princess." Josh MacDonald, the trainer Robynn rode for, took hold of the colt's bridle. "I've entered the two of you in the third race day after tomorrow. If it clears off like it looks like it might, you've got a real good chance."

"Thanks." Robynn pulled herself back to the moment. "He really feels ready." She concentrated on the white-haired man walking beside them. Tingles no longer tantalized the edges of her mind.

Robynn kicked her feet free of the stirrups and slid to the cedar shaving–covered walk in front of the long row of stalls belonging to Opal McKecknen. As Robynn unhooked the cinch to the tiny racing saddle, her mind flicked back to the stranger at the fence. *Wonder who he is? Why haven't I seen him around before?* Questions sparked like the dew glinting in his hair. That black hair. Crisp curls, cut short to control them. Control. The word fit him.

You idiot, she scolded herself. *You're acting like a dopey teenager, panting after every new boy on the block.*

No, not every one, she answered herself. *You've had the blinders on for seven years.*

"And I'll keep them on."

"What'd you say?" Josh finished cross-tying the steaming gelding.

"Nothing." Robynn shook her head. "I mean . . ."

"You all right?" The aging trainer lifted the saddle from her arms. "Ye're acting kinda strange."

"No. No. I'm fine. Or at least I will be when we get done with the workout. I'm so hungry I could eat burnt toast."

Josh handed her a scraper. "If you help me wash the horses down, I'll treat."

"You're on." Robynn stuck the scraper in the back pocket of her jeans.

clowning. "I'll have my usual, one boiled egg, four minutes, two slices wheat toast, dry."

"Thought you said you was hungry." Josh slid his tray down to the coffee urns. "Something about even burnt toast sounding good."

"That was before." She poured herself both a glass of orange juice and a steaming cup of coffee. "Let's sit over there." She pointed to any empty table in the far corner.

"Before what?" Josh removed his dishes from the tray and stacked both trays on another table. Robynn ignored him as she dug into the presectioned grapefruit. "Lady, you sure make an exciting meal partner." Josh buttered his pancakes after the waitress delivered their hot order. "A body'd think you was mad or something."

"Nope." Robynn smiled as she sipped her coffee. "Just following your instructions. Getting up for the race." *Liar,* the little voice perched on her shoulder scolded. *You can't get your mind off that stranger. Maybe you could find him again if you ran up and down the barns and around the track.*

"You gotta be kidding," she muttered under her breath.

"What'd you say?" Josh forked another bit of pancake into his mouth.

Robynn shook her head. "Nothing." She took a deep breath. "Nothing important."

"You know, if I didn't know you better . . ."

"Is this seat taken?" The stranger's voice was as deep as she knew it would be.

"Dane! You old coot!" Josh's chair slammed to the floor when he shoved it back. He ignored the crash as he leaped to his feet and, between hugs, pounded the newcomer on the back. "When'd you get here?"

"About an hour ago. Your string is looking good."

"Here." Josh pulled out the adjoining chair before righting his own. "Sit down, son, sit down."

Robynn felt like she'd come in at the middle of the second act at the theater. Everyone knew the action but her. One thing for certain: Her nervous system hit overload. There were no naps in sight for her nerve ends. To prove her exterior nonchalance, she reached for her just-refilled coffee cup. Sipping the scalding brew eased the crick in her neck earned while staring at the two ecstatic men.

Josh clapped a hand on her shoulder. "This here's my nephew, you know, the one from California. I told you about him before."

"The name's Morgan. Dane Morgan." Those startling blue eyes twinkled at Josh's chagrin. "This old buzzard forgot to tell you my name."

Robynn shook the proffered hand. And wished she hadn't.

"According to the man I asked," he continued, "they call you Princess."

Robynn nodded. She pulled her focus from the heat pulsing from her fingers to her wrist and up her arm. That same heat glued her tongue to the roof of her mouth. With precise concentration, she articulated a word in spite of her useless vocal cords. "Yes." Her inner voice was shocked into silence by her reaction. But only for a moment. *What in the world . . .* She could feel that voice gearing up for a full-blown assault.

Instead of listening, she searched Dane's eyes. They shimmered like high mountain lakes in the summer sun. When he smiled at her perusal, laugh lines crinkled at the corners of his eyes and white teeth emphasized his deep tan. A tan one would never find on anyone who lived in the Willamette Valley.

Abruptly he released her hand and with the easy grace of a man who knows his own body, settled into the chair next to her. "I watched you this morning. You ride well."

"She's one of the best." Josh winked at her. "I trained her just like I trained you."

"Do you have horses here?" Robynn straightened in her chair and tried for a friendly smile on her dry lips.

"Not yet." Dane leaned his elbows on the table. "I'm up here looking for a farm and another string of animals. Know any that are for sale?"

"Could be." Josh waved to the waitress to refill their cups. "In fact, there are several. You thinking of moving up here?"

"Yes. My company headquarters will remain in San Francisco, but I'm ready for something different. I need a new operation, and you've always raved about the Pacific Northwest, so here I am."

Robynn's eyes widened at the sheer arrogance of the man. She stared at Josh, willing him to look up at her.

Instead, he drew circles in the droplets of water on the Formica-topped table. "How big an operation you want?"

"Well, since it seems to me I paid for half of that Stealth fighter with my tax dollars alone, I know I need new shelters."

"Yeah, you and King Midas might be related . . ."

"Not quite. But things have gone well."

What an egotist. Robynn stared from one man to the other. Only sheer willpower kept her from laughing out loud. But they were serious. A tiny nod from Dane made her aware that her thoughts must be showing on her face again.

"You planning on moving your ponies up here?" Josh continued the discussion.

"All depends." Dane leaned back in his chair, teetering on the back two legs.

"On?"

"On what's available. It would be nice to race the entire coast season. I have an appointment with a Realtor in half an hour."

"You're planning on staying around for a time then?"

"Yes." Dane turned to Robynn, who carefully wiped the derision off her face. "I think I'm going to be around a lot."

"You about finished, Princess?" Josh seemed to stress the nickname. "We got a pile of work to do before the afternoon program."

Robynn nodded. "Nice to meet you, Dane." All her mother's schooling on company manners came to her aid. She smiled, a formal smile that tried to hide the mischief dancing in her eyes, as she pushed back her chair. Before she could finish the action, Dane was on his feet behind her. He pulled out her chair, making her feel like the royalty her name proclaimed. As she turned to leave, his hand on her arm stopped her.

"How about dinner tonight?" He turned her to face him.

Her gaze started at the mother-of-pearl snap midchest on his royal blue plaid western shirt, traveled up past the springy hair showing in the open V, paused at the cleft chin and smiling lips, and then locked into his direct gaze. The tingle from the ride earlier jangled a warning over her entire nervous system. Danger! Danger! It was as if a siren went off.

"I don't think so, but thank you anyway."

"Come on, Princess, he's safe. After all, he is my nephew." "But Josh." He knew she didn't date. What was the matter with him?

"Please." Since Josh rarely asked anything of her, his pleading look went straight to her heart.

"All right, I'd be glad to." She ignored the internal shock. *Glad to? Give me a break! I only said I'd go because Josh forced me.* She just barely kept herself from shaking her head.

"What time?" He obviously didn't waste words.

"I'll be done with chores after seven."

"Come on, Princess." Josh now commanded from the door. "We got work to do."

"Catch you later, Josh." Dane waved to his impatient relative. "Princess . . ." The deep timbre of his voice held her more securely than the hand burning her arm. "What about lunch? I can be back by then."

"No." She shook her head. "No time. Why?"

"I'd like to see you."

"But you said dinner."

"I know. But that's hours away."

"You don't let any grass grow under your feet, do you?" Robynn took a deep breath, hoping to calm the quivers his nearness ignited. Instead, the tang of expensive aftershave tickled her nose.

"No, I don't. When I see something I want, I go after it."

"I've got to get to work." Robynn's voice softened in spite of herself, mesmerized by the force he exuded.

"Coffee?"

"If you bring it to the tack room at noon." She fled to the barns, hooting in amazement at her reactions. *He'll never show. Men with a line like that never do.*

Sucker! I thought you were off women for the duration. Dane would like to have throttled the little voice laughing hysterically on his shoulder. True, he had decided to relax by searching for a new racing string and possible farm in the Pacific Northwest. True, he had given up in the quest for that perfect mythical mate in spite of his mother's pleading. And true, he had informed all friends and family to quit playing matchmaker. He slid into the seat of his silver Porsche. *Think I'll keep that appointment this morning short. There's plenty of time this afternoon. Wonder where she'd like to go for dinner?*

Mucking out stalls was not a job requiring any degree of concentration. It left Robynn with too much time to think, to remember. The pain was always there, just buried under the experiences of seven years of balancing a life at the track with the pain of widowhood and long-distance motherhood. Most days she wasn't sure which was worse. She could still see, hear, feel the day her husband left.

"I can't handle it," was all the slim-hipped, happy-go-lucky jockey had said. "I know I've not been that great a husband, but I'm definitely not cut out to be a daddy. You know that. See ya, kid." He grinned his heart-stopping smile, touched three fingers to his slouch hat, and roared off in his red Corvette.

The next day that same grin greeted her from the sports section of the evening paper: *Sonny O'Dell, Top Jockey at Portland Meadows.* A day later, the same paper carried the story of his wasted death, mangled and twisted within the frame of his 'Vette. Along with the girl who rode beside him . . . a real celebration they'd had.

At eighteen she'd wanted to run, to find someplace that had no memories of Sonny. Giving up seemed an appropriate response. But the baby growing inside her deserved a chance in spite of his parents' messed-up lives, so Robynn got on with living. She bought a house with part of the insurance money so she could make a home for their son. Jeremy she called him from the first fluttering movements. While the birth wasn't easy, the moment she first held her squirming little son in her arms was a thrill like nothing else in life. He was part of her, a new person to be surrounded with all the love her heart yearned to offer. Two months later, the doctors confirmed something Robynn suspected. Jeremy was blind. She dug in for the long stretch. Handicap was a word only for the racetrack. It would not stigmatize her son.

So much for the happily-ever-after kind of life the media promised. Without her friends and family, life would have seemed like happily-never-after. But she was a survivor. Jeremy would be, too. Her mother reminded her far more often than she appreciated that letting God help her would ease the pain, but the daughter would have none of it. If God cared so much, why was Jeremy born blind? If her mother wanted to pray—fine, but Robynn had no desire to return to the God of her youth, the God who had let her down so badly.

"What is it, Princess?" Robynn jumped as Josh touched her arm. Her wheelbarrow stopped with a thump. One look at her pain-punished eyes, and the trainer hustled her into an empty stall. "What's wrong? Something happen to Jeremy?"

"No. I saw him yesterday. He's fine. I just started thinking back, and that awful pain grabbed me again. It's always back there, just waiting. . . . Oh, Josh, why won't it go away. permanently?" Tears shimmered at the corners of her eyes.

"Ach, lass . . ."

"And part of it *is* Jeremy. I hate leaving him down at that school."

"But you'n' the counselors figured it was for the best . . ."

"Sure. The best school. The best training. But I only see him once a week and on vacations. Mothers are supposed to be there when their kid needs them. To tuck him in at night, to listen to his prayers. To kiss away his hurts."

"But you can't ride the circuit and drag him along. And you know he needs special training, consistently. At least for a while."

"I know all that. But still, I keep wondering. Am I doing what's best for him? Maybe I should take some office job so I can be home at regular hours." She stared at the dirt floor for an endless moment. When she raised her face, a single tear had escaped and glistened down her curved cheek.

Josh reached out with one gnarled finger and wiped the drop away. They'd been over this many times before.

"Come on, lass. You're supposed to be gettin' up for the race."

"I know." She took a deep breath, and like lifting a shade, her eyes cleared, her chin assumed its usual determined angle. Shoulders back, another chest-expanding breath, and the "Princess" took over again. "Thanks." Even the royal smile returned. "Don't be a'worryin' yerself, auld man." Her brogue thickened to distract him.

"Well, you'd be tellin' me if anything was to happen?" Bushy white brows met over his eyes. "Wouldn't ye?"

"Yes." Her shoulders sagged. "Yes. I promise."

Josh stared hard into her eyes for another millennium-like second, then turned and strode out of the stall. Robynn heard something like, "If I could just a-got my hands on that fool O'Dell . . . ," all muttered under his breath.

"Whew." Robynn breathed deeply, shrugging the cloud away. *You know better than to look back,* her inner voice scolded. *It never does any good. You swore to look forward, look only at the good things that are happening.* In a flash she saw blue eyes and hair glistening like the breast of a warbling blackbird. She sighed. *Definitely one of the good things.*

But then . . . no men, the little voice continued. *You said no man would ever cause you pain again. This one certainly could be painful if this flash of attraction is any indication. See, and you thought attraction like this only happened in the movies.*

Robynn finished dumping the loaded wheelbarrow and trundled it back to the tack room.

"Here." A steaming Styrofoam cup seemed to leap from the dimness and came to rest in her hand.

"Oh! You startled me." She leaned her back against the doorjamb, waiting for her heart to resume its normal beat. Without conscious thought, her body assumed a languid air. An errant sunbeam warmed her high cheekbones and sparked diamonds in the tendrils of hair that escaped the confining comb.

"You said noon." The shadowed stall made him loom even larger than before.

"And you're always punctual, I suppose."

"My middle name. Dane Punctual Morgan. Sounds good, don't you think? Nobody gave me a name like Princess."

Robynn eyed his blatantly masculine physique. "I should hope not. Princess would never suit you."

Dane chuckled, the warmth in his voice drawing them closer. "But it does suit you." He studied her over the rim of his coffee cup. "I think you stepped right out of a fairy-tale book."

A slight tremor shook her hand as Robynn set her half-empty cup on a shelf. The urge to stay and hear more fought with her awareness of the passing time.

"I've got to get going." She glanced a second time at the slim, silver band on her wrist. "Thanks for the coffee."

"The chores are done. Why don't you come with me instead?"

A look like he had misplaced his marbles crossed her face.

She shook her head. "Sorry, but I have races to run."

"I thought, hoped you just trained for Josh. You race?"

Robynn nodded.

"Take care, then."

Robynn had no idea how heartfelt his light comment really was.

Dane watched her leave. Slowly he ran his finger around the rim of his Styrofoam coffee cup. Riding was dangerous for anyone, but much more so for women. Why'd she . . .

"She's been bad hurt." Josh hung a horse sheet on the rack.

"Racing?" Dane's eyebrows shot up.

"No," Josh snorted. "By a man. She can handle the horses."

Keeping further questions to himself, Dane glanced at his watch. "See you this evening. I gotta run. And Josh, thanks for the info."

Why would anyone hurt her? The question nagged him as he strode out to the parking lot. What kind of fool had she been mixed up with?

The sun played tag with the low-floating clouds, more often than not losing the contest, as Robynn lugged her gear across the infield of the race track. Flags from the holes in the nine-hole golf course that utilized the infield snapped in the breeze. Spectators were already filing into the glass-enclosed grandstand in preparation for the day's entertainment, while the last golf cart putted out the gate.

Robynn turned and walked backwards on the sandy passage, checking to see if Mount Hood had received a fresh dusting of snow. The sharply pointed peak to the south of the broad Columbia River promised skiing in the winter. Poor, decapitated Mount St. Helens off to the north had never looked the same since the devastation from the volcano's eruption.

Seeing both mountains before a race was one of Robynn's good luck charms. She always won when both peaks were visible.

"I knew today felt good," she whispered. "A special day. A winning day." She turned, breathing deeply in the crisp clean air, not sullied with even a trace of pollution from the paper mills upriver. "Yes, a winning day." She turned for a last glimpse of the mountains, then with a light step crossed the track to the tunnel leading to the saddling area and the jockeys' locker rooms. With an effort she banished the image of broad, sheepskin-clad shoulders and a laughing grin.

Robynn blinked as the dimness of the concrete entry closed around her. After following the fenced area that kept spectators from getting too close to the horses in the saddling paddock, she opened the door to the weighing room and jockeys' locker rooms. Even the ancient green paint failed to dull her mood.

"Hey, Princess," one of the guys hailed her. "You up in the first?"

"Yeah, number six for Dr. Benson." She paused by the scale. "What about you?"

"Naw. Second race. All you old-timers get first choice."

Robynn grinned at the familiar complaint of the apprentice jockey. "I served my time," she reminded the young man not yet out of the acne stage. "You'll get yours, if you hang around long enough." She smiled at him again and turned left to the cramped dressing space for the women. Her nose wrinkled as the familiar aromas of liniment, shampoo, wet showers, and stale cigarette smoke assailed her upon opening the door. Half of the small room was taken up by the table for the resident chiropractor, who would bend and stretch the women on the table to get them in shape for the riding ahead. Benches lining the room were scattered with articles of tack and clothing.

"Hi, Princess." The girl on the chiropractor's table waved one hand, then grunted as the doctor snapped another vertebra into place.

"Still feeling the effects of that fall?" Robynn asked as she hung up her jacket.

"Ummm-hummm." The girl nodded. "I think we got clipped, or he wouldn'ta gone down like that. You watch that Romero. Talk about us women taking chances."

"Thanks for the advice. He's pretty young."

"Yeah, and money hungry. Let alone swamped by dreams of glory." She rolled onto her side. "You just be careful."

As Robynn wrapped a towel around her head and stepped into the showers, she could hear old Josh. *Keep your distance as much as you can,* he always said. *So your mount don't bang the horse's feet in front of you. That's clipping. You gotta watch who's coming up behind, too, so he don't do the same to you. Racing ain't just runnin' that nag around the track to win. You gotta develop a sixth sense about where everyone is and what they're likely to do. That's what makes a good jockey.*

Another voice and face took over her inner musings when she turned off the shower and wrapped herself in the emerald bath sheet. A face with angular planes, interesting shadows, and a well-used smile that crinkled up to his eyes. She'd already memorized that face well, even though she'd just met Dane that morning. Or had they known each other for eternity?

She could feel the rustle of her azure silk dress as it swished against her legs. First dinner, then ...

"Hey, Princess!" A voice next to her shattered her vision. "If you're up in the first, you better quit daydreaming and get a hustle on."

TWO

*D*ane thumped a fist on the steering wheel as he threaded the Porsche through the traffic on the way to the Realtor's office. He hadn't been impressed with the man he'd met that morning. The woman he'd spoken with later sounded suitably enthusiastic. After he'd outlined what he wanted, she promised to show him several farms.

His frustration increased as he found himself caught behind a slow-moving truck. Why'd she have to be a jockey? Training and exercising weren't so bad. Accidents were rare in the morning hours. But he'd seen some bad ones during the program; races when both riders and horses had died. Living with a mother permanently crippled during a steeplechase taught him another side of the tragedy of accidents.

And I didn't keep her safe.

He thumped the wheel again. Women should *not* be licensed as jockeys. No matter how good they were. Sheer strength counted at times. While he knew his views were considered chauvinistic in today's world, he had no intention of changing his mind.

He gunned the Porsche past the dump truck. His mother's voice came back to him. *You're acting like a chauvinist, Son.* But then, she hadn't been a spectator as he had while the pain she experienced drove the son to curse the cause. She should have been in the grandstand that fateful day, rather than in the racing saddle. He should have made sure of that, like his father had commanded him.

He switched off the dark thoughts along with the car key. Sliding from the low-slung car, he strode toward the real estate office. Now was the time to concentrate on his future. He took a deep breath and blinked hard to dispel the vision of laughing, violet eyes.

By the time the call came for weighing in, Robynn's resident troop of butterflies cavorted in aerial shows in her stomach. Today was a four-star performance no matter how many times she swallowed and ordered them back to their roosts.

"One hundred five pounds." The scale master handed her seven pounds of lead to insert in the slots of her saddle pad. "That brings you up to the one hundred twelve you need. Have a good one." He grinned at her. "Next."

Robynn paused a moment to scan the crowd across the entry to the paddock, hoping, in spite of what he'd said, to see a tall man in a sheepskin jacket. Instead, she grinned and waved at an appreciative wolf whistle. Even with her wavy hair tucked up under her green, silk-covered racing helmet, no one could mistake her for one of the guys. The loose-fitting silks failed to conceal her slender neck and shoulders. Silky white pants curved from her narrow waist over slim but definitely feminine hips and down long legs to be tucked into knee-high riding boots. Self-assurance, obvious in the tilt of her determined chin, belied the fluttering horde of butterflies halfway up her throat.

All the horses were already in the individual stalls that spoke-wheeled from a central hub in the cavernous saddling paddock. Robynn circled to the right until she found her mount for this race. She had ridden the horse several times before, once to a second place.

Mounted on Tame Adventure, she listened to the last minute instructions of the trainer. Finally he led the animal out to the pony riders, who led the Thoroughbreds around the track to the starting gate.

Her mount broke clean at the gate and easily swept into the lead, winning by a length. "You did it, old man." She patted the horse's steaming shoulder as she turned him back toward the winner's circle. "Good fella." The horse side-stepped his way through the spectators to stand in front of the cameras. Robynn slipped her saddle off his back as the officials draped a horseshoe wreath of red and white roses over his withers.

"Congratulations." Portly Dr. Benson pumped her hand. "You two looked really good out there."

"Thank you." Robynn smiled for the flash camera and, while searching the crowd for certain blue eyes, finished her conversation. "Tame Adventure was really ready, and so was I. You have a good horse there."

"Let's just hope this is the first of many." The doctor beamed.

Robynn smiled her agreement and stepped on the scale. A feeling of discontent niggled at her mind. Where was he? Maybe she'd been wrong. Maybe he didn't feel the same way she did. But it sure felt both ways at the time. And he *had* asked her out to dinner. But he didn't even know where she lived. The internal argument never showed on her smiling face.

By the end of the day, Robynn felt like she'd been run over by a Mack truck. Every muscle ached, and even though she'd been in the money four times, including two firsts, the hovering miasma of disappointment refused to dissipate.

"You did a good job with that gray." Josh nodded as she returned to the stalls. "Never dreamed he'd make it into the money."

"I hate to say 'I told you so' but . . ."

"Then don't. Park your hunkus on that chair for a spell." He pointed to the director's chair in the corner of the tack room. "You look like your best friend took a hike."

Robynn sat as ordered, glad of the opportunity to let down.

She leaned back into the curving canvas and, with closed eyes, allowed the tiredness and the black mood to seep out through her booted toes.

"Whyn't you just head on home," Josh said, pity for the purple shadows under her closed eyes evident in his glance. "You look done in."

"What about feeding?"

"I'll manage. Been taking care of horses long before you came along."

"Thanks, Josh." The weary woman rose to her feet. "You're a real friend." She paused at the door. "If anyone should ask for me . . ."

"I'll tell him."

Robynn nodded.

The drive to her house out by Portland State passed in a blur of stops and starts. Her black Celica shifted easily and turned as if it knew the way without her assistance. Even the bronze and fiery red chrysanthemums lining her driveway failed to lift her spirits in their customary way. She unlocked the back door and, as she closed it, dropped her jacket, then sweater and shirt on her way to the bathroom. Once in the bedroom, she rammed her heel into the bootjack by her bed and, after straining to pull the boots off, flung each one in the general direction of the closet. "I'll clean them later," she promised herself as she staggered to the shower.

Minutes later Robynn slipped between cool sheets and pulled the navy down comforter up to her chin. Flashing blue eyes dominated her thoughts as she sighed her way into dreamland. *She and Dane, sitting across from each other at a restaurant. Their eyes locked. He moved his hand across the table to capture hers. There were flames from his touch; his breath, teasing her ear as he leaned forward, sent wind-blown sparks igniting brushfires wherever they lit. The music played countermelody to the blood pulsing through her limbs, drugging her mind.*

A buzzing—long, then short—wended its way through the rhythm. The buzz disrupted the dance, the man in her arms faded as if she watched the action through the wrong end of a telescope.

"Buzzzzzz." That nagging presence sounded again. Still in the rosy warmth of the land between waking and sleeping, Robynn knotted the belt of her royal purple robe at her waist and drifted for the front entrance. Just as an impatient finger pressed the doorbell again, she twisted the lock and swung open the door.

"Yes-s-s." Her eyes and mouth O'd as she clutched her robe more tightly around her. "D-Dane." *Oh ground, swallow me up right now!*

"Last time I looked in the mirror that's who I was."

"I . . . ah . . . I'm not ready."

"I can tell that." He leaned forward and lowered his voice. "Don't you think you should invite me in before your neighbors start to talk?"

She stepped back, the heat that fired up her neck making her wish for a fan—one powered high enough to blow this man right off the steps. She stepped back and beckoned him in. Pointing to the living room, she said in a rush. "You can wait in there." She turned and headed down the hall. "I'll just be a few minutes."

His "take your time," floated after her.

As if racing for the finish line, Robynn threw her clothes on the bed, not wasting time on the selection. With a swish, the deeply-draped neckline of her azure silk dress settled in place. She smoothed the full skirt over her hips and reveled as the fabric swirled about her legs. She loved silk, the fabric of royalty—especially princesses being taken to dinner.

A touch of dusky, gray-blue eye shadow and navy mascara set her eyes to shimmering as she outlined her perfectly bowed lips with deep rose lipstick. Peach blush emphasized her high cheekbones, and with a dusting of powder, she was finished. Swiftly she glanced over her collection of fragrances, her one feminine weakness. Which one could be termed romantic? She stared for a moment at her reflection in the mirror, grabbed a bottle of Shalimar, and sprayed it lightly on pulse points. The cut glass atomizer clinked as she set it down.

She started out of the room but stopped in front of the dresser that held her stand for pierced earrings. Only for a moment, she debated before choosing the tiny diamonds, her wedding present from . . .

Abruptly she attached them to the lobes of her ears and with a toss of the cloud of hair caressing her shoulders, flicked off the light and left the room. Pausing for a moment in the arched doorway, she unconsciously waited for a reaction from the man prowling her living room.

"Dane?"

He spun from his study of the wall decorated with framed photos of her in the winner's circle, candids of her favorite mounts, Josh and other track officials, plus a large color shot of an entire field of Thoroughbreds straining around the far turn of the track.

The now familiar tingle started at her toes and, like a Derby entry in the homestretch, raced to the top of her head.

"Princess?" Her name was a whisper on his lips as he blinked at the transition from racing to dining silks. The moment stretched until goose bumps crept up Robynn's arms from the intentness of his gaze.

"I'm ready."

"Right." Dane Morgan seemed to recall himself from some far distant land as he stepped forward to take the coat she held. She slipped her arms in the coat sleeves as he held her coat for her. It had been so long since anyone held her coat. She sighed at the pleasure. His fingers sent curls of excitement coursing over her scalp when he lifted her hair from the neckline of her cream wool coat.

"Your chariot awaits." He squeezed her shoulders before opening the front door. "Your Highness."

Portland had donned her evening gown of lights as they cruised the wide street above the shipping center of Swan Island. The Fremont Bridge rose in all its white glory with the United States and Oregon flags snapping in the spotlights high above the crest. While the City of Roses was Portland's nickname, Robynn always felt City of Bridges would fit better, as five spans crossed the Willamette River in as many miles.

Skyscrapers from round to octagonal glittered in their formal evening dress, giving the city a distinctive skyline.

Robynn loved it all. Portland was a gutsy, growing metropolis with typical urban difficulties but room for a racetrack and breeding farms within twenty minutes of downtown.

"Where're we going?" She settled deeper into the rich leather seat of the silver Porsche.

"You'll know soon enough." Dane clicked a CD into the player. The clear tenor of John Denver's "Rocky Mountain High" filled the car.

Fifteen minutes later, after discovering mutual interests in music and food, they pulled up in front of Maggie's Olde Inn, one of Robynn's favorite restaurants.

Dane tucked her arm in his as they left the car and walked up the short flagstone path to the entry. Heavy wooden doors crossed with iron bands swung open when he pressed the latch.

Stepping inside was like walking through a time warp, back a hundred years to merry old England. Dark beams spanned the ceiling and led one's eyes to the focal point of the dining room, a man-sized fireplace set in the tabby wall. Waitresses in gathered skirts and white mobcaps rushed between the dark wooden tables surrounded by patrons.

"Two for Morgan," Dane responded to the hostess's query.

The svelte blond bypassed the main dining room and led them up a steep, narrow stair to an alcove just large enough for a table for two. Robynn could hear other diners in the individual rooms around them, but the illusion of privacy lent a mysterious air to the evening.

"Enjoy your dinner." The hostess stood two leather-bound menus in front of them. "Your waitress will be right up."

"Thanks."

Robynn took a deep breath. "Um . . ." She paused, trying to think. "How did you enjoy the races today?"

"I didn't."

"What?" Robynn shook her head.

"No, no. It's not what you think. I love horse racing."

Her held-in breath sent the candle flickering as it escaped.

"But I couldn't enjoy the races because I wasn't there." The twinkle in his eyes told her he knew what she'd thought. "I was out with that Realtor looking at farms. I told you I wanted to buy one."

"That's right. Did you see any good ones?"

"Nothing I really liked. But when I stopped by the track, Josh told me of one. He said his owner was thinking of selling out."

"Yes." Robynn sipped her iced tea again. "She's been ill."

"She?"

"Opal McKecknen. Her husband died several years ago. He was a really dedicated Thoroughbred breeder, but she loved the horses as much as he, so she kept the string going. Josh has done a good job for her. He oversees the farm and breeding stock besides running the training and racing here at the track."

"I have an appointment to talk with her tomorrow."

"It's really hard for her." Robynn frowned as she thought of the birdlike woman who rode well enough to have been a jockey herself. "Getting old is the pits."

"What do you think of Robynn O'Dell?" His question caught her by surprise.

"Um—m—m—m . . . that's . . ."

Before she could gather her wits enough to finish the sentence, Dane interrupted. "All the track was talking about him, how well he did today."

Robynn took a swallow of ice water to dispel the rock in her throat. He didn't know who she was. She stared at him, hoping to find a teasing light in his eyes. None.

"I'll need a man like that."

"Uh—h, there are other good jockeys out there, too." Robynn felt caught in a trap. "We're finding that many times women make better riders."

"No." Dane stated an absolute. "Not for me. I'll never have a woman up on one of my horses during a race."

THREE

Robynn's inner warmth dropped to below zero. The tingles turned to icicles. "Did I hear you right?" Each word seemed sheathed in ice.

"What's the matter?" Dane shook his head, question marks all over his face. "I don't have anything against women exercising horses. But racing is too dangerous. Women just don't have the strength to control half a ton of hurtling horseflesh."

"And men do?"

"Well, not always." She could see he was trying to be honest. "But at least they have a better chance."

"And how many horses have *you* raced?"

"None. Princess, I don't understand—"

"Don't call me that!" Her chin had turned to steel, matching the glint in her eyes.

"What . . . ?"

"Princess." Her tone was flat. "Mr. Morgan, do you know what my name is? My real name?"

He stared at her. The silence lengthened, taut as a guitar string turned once too many times. "No. I don't guess I do."

"My name is Robynn, as in Robynn O'Dell." She watched as his eyes narrowed. "You said earlier, you wanted to hire me?"

"O—h—h . . ."

"Surprised? And I'll let you in on a little secret, Mr. Fancy Horse Buyer from California. I wouldn't ride for you if you owned Citation, Seattle Slew, *and* Man O' War." She rose. Queen Elizabeth couldn't have been more regal. "And now, I find I've lost my appetite. Do you want to take me home or shall I call a cab?"

"Princess!" The ice in her eyes reminded him. "All right, Robynn. I didn't know. You're a good rider."

"Just not good enough for your horses, the horses . . ." Her control cracked around the edges.

"No, that's not what I meant. Sit down so I can talk to you." He tried to stare her down. "You could have told me your real name. Not just let me run on like some babbling fool."

"If the shoe fits?" Robynn could see she'd gone about as far as was wise. Straight, black brows met at the scowl furrows in his forehead. His hand clenched and unclenched on the handle of the coffee mug. Anger burned from his eyes, furnace-hot rather than icy.

"Sit down!" Each consonant snapped like a rifle shot. Robynn didn't move. "The cab?"

"No! I'll take you home." He grabbed his jacket and rammed his arms into the sleeves. This time when he held her coat, his fingers felt like they'd rather pull her hair than lift it gently. *Pull it out by the roots, most likely,* she thought. The way he hustled her down the stairs and threw some bills at the astounded waitress left Robynn in no doubt of his feelings.

"Have a good evening." The door slammed on the hostess's words.

"I am strong enough to make it to the car on my own." Robynn tried to slow him down, but the fingers clenched on her upper arm forced her to dogtrot in her high heels. "Even if I am a woman." Honey dripped from her change in tone.

Dane Morgan didn't seem to like the sweetness any better than the ice as he stuffed her into the silver Porsche.

The drive to her home passed in a silence so loud it hurt her ears. She stepped out of the car before he could open his door when the vehicle halted in her driveway. Her stiff "thank you" was lost in the roar of the engine as Dane rammed the machine into reverse and shot back into the street.

"Well, my girl," Robynn said to herself as she swung open the front door. "It sure felt good for a while. But . . ." She hung her coat in the closet. "You better stick to horses and small boys." She wandered into the bedroom and picked up the latest picture of Jeremy, framed against the backdrop of the State School for the Blind. "You seem to do better in those categories." She studied the sweet face of her son. "Oh Jeremy, I miss you so. And thanks to that *gentleman,* I didn't get to call you tonight. What a mistake." She set the picture back down and sighed.

She could feel the anger resurging. "What a stupid, chauvinistic attitude. Men!" She dropped her earrings on the dresser top. "At least, this time *I* did the dumping. And before I got hurt."

As she slipped between the sheets, electric blue eyes flashed back on her inner vision. *At least, I hope so.* The small voice sounded doubtful.

All the tossing and turning made inroads on Robynn's alertness for the morning. She woke up feeling drained and out of sorts and she hadn't recovered her normal good humor by the time she reached the stables. Liquid sunshine, as Portlanders call their frequent rain, misted her hair and dripped onto her neck, only adding to her depression.

"You seem down," Josh commented after watching her mope around the tack room, waiting for the horses to finish their grain.

"Yeah. To get even with a pregnant centipede, I'd have to reach up."

"That bad, huh?"

"Must be the rain."

"How is Dane this morning, or rather last night?"

She stared at the knowing twinkle in his eyes.

"Well, when he left here, he seemed mighty anxious to find your house. I just assumed . . ."

"Well, you know what assuming does. And I'm not the one to feel like a you-know-what this morning." The words poured faster as her anger returned.

"And ye're meaning he should?"

"Meaning that he wanted to hire the great Robynn O'Dell to ride his future horses until he found out Robynn O'Dell is me!"

"Hold on now, lass." Josh shook his head. "Ye're not making a lot of sense."

"Josh, he doesn't want a woman jockey. Afraid I can't handle these *huge* animals in a real race." She whirled from the far wall she'd been staring into. "I'd like to show him how strong . . ."

"He hasn't seen you race." Josh picked up a saddle and sat down on a bale of hay to start the never-ending cleaning.

"No. And I don't care if he ever does."

"Lass, he has an appointment with Opal McKecknen today." Josh rubbed the rag around the can of saddle soap and applied the cream to the leather.

"I know. And that's what scares me silly." She joined him on the hay bale.

"We've been a team for a long while." Josh patted her shoulder. "But you can ride for anyone now. That agent of yours'll have half the owners beating down his door after your wins this last week. You were somethin' to see."

"But ... but ..." She paused, trying to straighten out the thoughts careening through her brain. "It's like Opal's horses are my own. I've been with some of them since they were dropped. I broke and trained them. I want to keep on riding them, besides the others."

"Here." He handed her the rag and saddle. "Might as well be useful, 'stead of flittin' about."

Robynn continued the circular motions without a break. Her brow furrowed while she stared unseeing at the leather in her hands. The turning wheels could nearly be heard out loud as her agile brain shifted into high gear.

"Josh, Opal is serious about selling?"

"Um." He continued soaping a headstall. The squeak of leather in his hands grew loud in the silence.

Concentrating so hard on the ideas bursting in her mind, Robynn stared intently at the saddle in her lap. "Let's buy them."

"Them, who?"

"The horses. Our horses."

"Are ye daft, girl? Where'd we be gettin' that kind of money?"

"You said it yourself, we've been partners for a long time. This way we could be real partners." She dumped the half-cleaned saddle as she sprang to her feet. "Then I could keep riding them. Before Dane buys the whole shootin' match from her."

"But, Princess, we don't know for sure he's gonna buy them."

"How can he help it? He seems to have the money." With an impatient hand, she brushed back the raven wings of hair on her temples. "You know what a perfect setup it is. And besides, if not him, then someone else will."

Unbidden, thoughts of the McKecknen farm leaped into her consciousness. A split rail fence surrounded the sprawling brick ranch house. Next to the newly painted white stables, the quarter-mile track made breaking and training convenient. Acres of lush pasture dotted with grazing Thoroughbreds proclaimed the set purpose of the place. The sturdy sign with the words "McKecknen's Racing Stables" painted in green only made it official.

It was truly a horse and rider heaven. And in her mind, on the trail that circled back into the fir trees on the hills behind the farm, trotted two riders. Herself and a broad-shouldered, ebony-headed man. Laughter floated on the breeze. Knees brushed as they rode side by side, and at the spot where the alder trees kissed overhead, they stopped.

Robynn shook her head, bringing herself back to the tack room and her conversation with Josh.

"That it be. Yeah, it be that perfect." The deep crevices in his forehead revealed more than his words.

"I know I could take out a loan against my house."

"What about the payments to Jeremy's school?"

"They'd come from somewhere. I've never borrowed from my parents before. Dad might get real excited about owning part interest in the ponies." Robynn's words tumbled over themselves in her excitement.

"Whoa, lass." The old man waved a hand in front of her nonfocusing eyes. "Yer like a filly with the bit in her teeth. Slow down."

"I can't, Josh. I never thought of doing something like this before." She whirled at the corner and strode back across the room. A single lightbulb dangled on a cord from the ceiling, alternately casting shadows then highlights on her face as she paced. "You said it yourself. My agent will get plenty of mounts for me."

"Sounds like I said far too much, the way you keep turnin' my words agin me," Josh grumped at the bridle clutched in his aging fingers.

"She wouldn't want the money all at once." Robynn spun again, striding back and forth. "Would she?"

"Don't ask me." Josh hung the headstall and saddle back on the pegs in the wall. "I just work here."

Robynn stopped her pacing. "You don't think it could happen, do you?"

"Right now I think you better get out there and work them horses." He led the way to the door. "Before it's noon."

"Josh!" She grabbed his arm. "Answer me."

Absently, he patted her fingers. "I dunno, lass. Ye've surprised me, that's all." He squinted up at the still-dripping heavens as if to receive instructions from above.

Robynn waited. All the early morning sounds of a track penetrated her consciousness. Down the line a horse nickered. Another whinnied, answering a call from across the barns. In the next stall, Tame Adventure banged the door with a pawing hoof, demanding his release. The pungent aroma of ammonia, straw, and horses filled her nostrils.

"All I can promise . . ." He patted her hand again. "Is to think about it. To really think about it."

"You've always dreamed of owning a string of Thoroughbreds," she whispered. "You know you have."

"You take Finding Fun out first." He pointed to the sorrel filly with her head hanging over the stall door. "Work her easy for a couple a miles, then breeze her for two furlongs. We'll clock her and see how she's comin' along. I'd like to enter her in that maiden race next week."

Robynn knew better than to keep pushing him. When Josh promised to think about something, she knew he would, slowly and carefully, searching every angle.

All the animals seemed bathed in a new light as she looked at them through the eyes of a possible future owner. She knew all their strengths and weaknesses, how to outsmart their quirks, how to get the best from them. Between her and Josh, they might as well have owned the string as it was—Opal had let them have such a free hand the last year. But then both Opal and her husband had depended completely on Josh to train and manage their horses and breeding farm, even before Mr. McKecknen died.

Finding Fun was one of Robynn's favorite animals. She had been at the farm the day the filly entered the world, snorting and kicking. Feisty Fun would have been a good name for her. Her inquisitive nose was always into anything new, but while she pushed and tried each restraint, she'd never been mean.

"I can't wait to race you." Robynn rubbed the white blaze on the filly's nuzzling nose. "You've got the speed and the heart. Now all you need is the experience." The filly nodded as if she agreed. Robynn chuckled while she snapped the cross ties onto the soft web halter.

After they'd groomed the filly, Josh boosted Robynn into her saddle. "You remember what I said about this workout?"

Robynn nodded down at him and lowered her goggles into place.

"Fine, then. I'll be up in the bleachers, so let her out at the pole in front."

Robynn calmed the dancing filly. "Josh." She tightened the reins even more. "You won't talk to anyone about our discussion this morning, will you?"

"Ach, lass, ye know me better'n that." He led the animal toward the track entrance.

She smiled and patted the filly's shoulder. "You're right. I think I just needed to hear myself talk." As she rode out onto the track, the drizzling mist muffled the hoofbeats of the other horses working the sandy oval. Across the field the grandstand seemed fuzzy, its outline slightly out of focus, blurred by the gloom.

Robynn tried to keep her mind on the animal she was riding, but the smooth canter the filly settled into lulled her into thinking about the evening before. The time with Dane had felt so good. Even their senses of humor were compatible. All except for the fact that he was a totally insufferable, close-minded . . . She slammed her mental door on the memories. As she and her mount swept easily past the gate on their first mile, she felt the now familiar tingle. "Dummy!" She scolded herself. "Even just thinking about him causes a reaction. This has got to stop."

The next time around, though, she scanned the small covered and heated bleachers where owners and trainers could get out of the rain to watch the workouts. Beside Josh, in the middle row, a sheepskin jacketed figure leaned against the wooden bench behind them. One lazy hand lifted in greeting.

Robynn's hands loosened on the reins as her mind went into shock. Instantly aware of her rider's lack of concentration, the filly snorted and leaped forward. The jolt brought Robynn back to the present with a snap. Reflex action kept her in the saddle and had her back in control before they'd gone four more paces.

Good reaction time, she congratulated herself after her heartbeat returned to normal. *Good reaction time, my foot,* her resident critic chided. *You nearly blew that one, and all because of that man. You know, the one you said would never bother you.* Robynn mentally turned off the voices and leaned forward to pat the filly's shoulder.

"Never a dull moment with you around, is there?" Her voice gentled the excited filly. But when they reached the pole again, the horse leaned into the bit, asking for more rein. "Come on, baby! Go for it!"

The filly didn't need a second invitation. Within two paces, Finding Fun leveled out, each stride increasing her speed.

Robynn loved the speed and power so much she nearly forgot to pull up at the appointed post. "Another time, girl." Robynn leaned her weight against the reins as globs of lather splattered her from the heaving animal. As they neared the gate, Josh waved them over.

Robynn refused to meet the eyes of the man towering over Josh. Instead she beamed at her trainer. "Good, huh?" She pushed her goggles up on her helmet.

"Seventeen and a half. She sure can move." Josh stroked the filly with one hand while he held the bridle with the other. "Had a hard time getting her to stop, didn't ye?"

"Some." Robynn grinned down at him. "But she minded anyway." While the two of them discussed the ride, the tingles sprinting up and down her spine reminded her that another man stood beside the filly's head. Deliberately she kept her gaze on the trainer. At the same time, her back straightened, the tilt of her chin assumed its imperial angle.

"Well, let's get the mud off her and cool her out." Josh headed to the barn.

As Robynn nudged the filly to follow, a tanned hand grasped the reins just under the horse's jaw. "Robynn . . ."

She stared out between the sorrel ears, the exhilaration of the run evaporating. She glared down at the hand he placed on her knee. The icicles returned to spike her words."Excuse me, I don't—"

"I'm sorry I acted the way I did last night." Dane interrupted her before she could go any farther. He removed his hand.

Robynn could hear and feel the ice shattering like an unexpected spring thaw.

"Can we please agree to disagree?" His contrite tone forced her to look at him. "Please forgive me."

"Yes." Her response caught her by surprise.

Violet eyes locked with sky blue. Robynn forgot the rain, the run, and the dampness creeping down her neck. It was as if the sun had forced its way through the clouds to shine just on them. The glow spread from the spot on her knee where his hand had been, leaped to her mouth to tug at its corners, and danced on up to twinkle in her eyes.

She spoke around the ripple of laughter in her throat. Iridescent notes of joy burst from the prison in her chest and winged their way to find the sun. "We can try to do that."

"And Robynn." He leaned against the nudge the impatient filly gave him.

"My friends call me Princess," she interrupted him softly.

"Friends." He held out his right hand.

"Friends." She placed her own in his. She had to breathe deeply to counteract the shock of the pressure of his fingers around hers.

Finding Fun raised her head, pulling against the weight of the hand on her reins. When another nudge failed to catch their attention, she jigged sideways, staring imploringly toward the barn.

With another smile, Dane turned and led them up the road.

"I'll take her now," Josh said as they reached the row of stalls. Nodding, Robynn kicked out of the stirrups and, swinging her right leg over the filly's rump, slid to the ground. She turned and bumped into a solid wall of male chest.

"What time are you done today?"

It was the last question she expected. "Why?"

"Two things. I'd like you to look at some farms with me. You know the area, and that way you'll know what I'm looking for."

"And?"

"And I'd like to take you out to dinner again. To make up for last night. Some subjects we just won't discuss right now, okay?"

Can I really do this? Agree to disagree and not bring up the subject that means so much to me? Lord, if this is from You, aren't You asking an awful lot of me? The silence lengthened before she finally sighed.

"Right." She nodded as if to seal the bargain. "And now I'd better get back to work or Josh'll come looking for me."

"Speaking of angels . . ."

"Is that what you call him?"

Josh thrust the reins of the bay Come Runnin' in her hands. "Someone around here better get some work done or they'll be blowing Parade before we're finished." He winked at her when he saw the sunlight smile on her face. "Looks like we bypassed the centipedes."

I hope so, Robynn thought. *I'm tired of feeling down.*

Well, you've got a lot to look up to now, her sneaky little voice giggled. *Dane Morgan is pretty big and . . .* Robynn pulled her goggles into place and swung her mount out on the track. The mist blew in her face. Surprised, she licked the moisture from her lips. She'd thought sure the sun was shining.

FOUR

By three o'clock when Robynn finished riding for the day, she probably wouldn't remember which horse she won with and which placed third. For sure she'd put the loser out of her mind. She'd used all her powers of concentration during each race, but between them—

"Princess," the scale master had chided, "don't you think you'd better have the silks on your helmet match your shirt? Most owners appreciate that kind of uniform." Robynn dashed back to change, the red staining her cheeks not a reflection from the silks she wore.

The other women jockeys kept out of her way as Robynn broke the sound barrier showering and dressing. Impatiently she tucked the turquoise silk blouse into the waistband of black western pants, then pulled the lacy black v-neck sweater over her head. By the time she added silver earring loops and two chains, Robynn the woman was metamorphosed from Robynn the jockey. The addition of mauve eye shadow and black mascara, plum lipstick and blusher completed the transition.

"It's just not fair," grumbled one of the women.

"What's not?" Robynn halted the brush sweeping the waves back in her hair.

"You're not only a fantastic rider, but you walk out of here looking like a model."

"At five feet, three inches?" Robynn snorted. "Some model. I could maybe pose for the junior wear."

"Well, it's just not fair."

"Thanks." Robynn finished brushing her hair, shrugged into her leather hip-length jacket, and slung her duffel over her shoulder. "You make me feel good."

The wolf whistle from one of the fans that greeted her as she stepped out the door added even more to her self-confidence. But the look in Dane's eyes caused the roses to bloom on her cheeks.

"The wait was worth every minute." The tang of wood burning stoves greeted them as they stepped onto the parking lot. The three-story structure with the lighted sign above showing perpetually running horses dominated the flatlands of Delta Park, now being taken over by retail stores, hotels, and light industry.

"This way." Dane took her elbow to guide her through the puddles left from the earlier rain.

Even through her jacket, Robynn could feel the warmth from his hand. But the heat that radiated from his touch had nothing to do with body temperature.

This is crazy, Robynn scolded herself. *One touch and your pulse is racing like Finding Fun in the homestretch. You've been out with good-looking guys before.*

A–a–a–h, a countervoice responded. *But the chemistry is here. You've never met someone with chemistry like this between the two of you. Not even with Sonny. This can lead to something special.*

"Are you hungry?" Dane's deep voice interrupted the small voices arguing in her brain.

"Not really. Are you?"

Dane opened the door to his Porsche and tossed her bag in the back. "Nope. But let's grab a pop as we go. Buckle your seat belt." He slammed the door and strode around the front of the car.

"Stupid thing." Robynn fussed with the black straps as Dane slid into his seat. "You need a master's degree in seat belts to ever figure them all out."

"Here, let me." Dane leaned across her, his shoulder brushing hers. Robynn froze. She sucked in her breath trying to make herself as small as possible, but the contact sent quivers to her middle.

Vaguely she realized it was taking longer than necessary to adjust the belt. At the final click, Dane turned his head. The grin that lifted the corners of his sharply etched lips slowly faded, but the twinkle in his eye invited an answer from hers.

Robynn blinked as he finally drew away, her long lashes raised to reveal violet eyes full of question marks.

"Dane—I . . ." *Was he about to kiss me? Or am I making things up?*

"You what?"

"I—I don't know you well enough to . . ."

"To?" He waited. "To what?" The twinkle returned. "To go have a pop with me?"

"No, you nut." The mood was broken, and Robynn wasn't sure if she was happy or sad—or somewhere in between. After all, she hadn't been kissed in a long, long time.

"Dane!" Robynn tried to keep a straight face but giggled instead. She settled back in her seat, contentment wrapped like a fleecy blanket around her. Being with this man felt so good.

"Here." He handed her a sheet of paper off the dash. "You be the navigator. I have no idea where we're going."

"Now I know why you brought me along. And here I thought it was because you wanted the pleasure of my company."

"Don't kid yourself, lady." Dane turned the key and the engine roared to life. "Another time and place and I'll show you just why I want you around."

"Dane."

"What?" He glanced in the rearview mirror and out both windows.

"Your seat belt." She pointed to the strap still hanging in place. "You want me to help you with it?"

Dane grinned at her innocent expression. "I think that's what got us into trouble before."

"I wouldn't call that trouble." She stared straight ahead, chewing her lip to keep from laughing at him.

"Where's the nearest watering trough?" The silver Porsche accelerated, spraying water from the puddles.

By the time they'd purchased two large Cokes at the hamburger stand and zoomed up the entrance to I-5, the north-bound lanes were already slowing with the afternoon's rush-hour traffic. Dane shifted down and eased into the bumper-to-bumper flow of homeward-bound cars.

"Freeways are the same everywhere, I guess." He paused while a madman changed lanes like no one else was around. "But compared to rush hour down south, this is a Sunday afternoon drive."

"I hear they're pretty bad. Especially down around LA."

"You ever been down in my country?"

"For vacations. You know. Rush down. See the high spots. And rush home again. My folks enjoyed taking their vacations in the southwest and along the coast."

"Your parents live around here?"

"U-m-m. Out in Lake Oswego. I'm a born and bred Oregonian. There aren't an awful lot of us around. Seems most everyone you meet is a transplant." She turned in her seat so she could watch him. "What about you?" His profile seemed even more strongly defined when viewed against the backdrop of steel girders as they crossed the Interstate Bridge. "Oh, get in the right-hand lane. Quick. We follow the signs to Camas."

"Now you tell me." Dane checked the cars around him and roared across two lanes. "Some navigator you are."

"Sorry." Robynn opened her eyes again. She'd squeezed them shut when the bumper of a service truck tried to peer in her window.

"You take that first exit, hard to the right." Robynn pointed as she spoke. "That puts you on Highway 14." After they navigated the turn, she asked, "What kind of farm are you looking for?" As soon as she asked it, she realized he hadn't told her anything about himself. It seemed that every time they talked, he asked her questions. Was he hiding something or what?

"About fifty to one hundred acres. Large house. I'd like to find one operational if I can. Otherwise I'll buy the land and build it the way I want. That'll take longer, though. I hate to wait."

"Have you thought of east of the mountains?"

"Looked into it. But that's too far from a good track. I was thinking of the Seattle area, too, until Longacres folded. But that uncle of mine has been filling my head with stories of how wonderful Portland is for more years than I can remember."

"It is wonderful," Robynn stated emphatically.

"That's prejudice. You've never lived anywhere else."

"Nope. And don't care to."

"Opinionated, aren't you?"

"My father always said, 'Know your mind and speak it—nicely, of course.'" Robynn studied the play of Dane's broad hands on the wheel of the powerful little car. The two seemed made of one piece, man and machine. "Do you ride much?"

"Some. I love to ride along the beach. Especially in the early morning or at sunset. Of course, I never seem to have time in between."

"That's something I've always wanted to do. Instead, we went horseback packing in the mountains. Dad loves the Cascade Crest trail." Robynn closed her eyes to remember the brisk mornings, high clear mountain lakes, and snow-capped lava peaks towering on either side of a rocky trail.

"You took your own horses?"

"No. I've never owned a horse. That's one of my major, major dreams."

"How'd you get into racing then?"

"Just showed up at the track one day, willing to do anything so I could be around the horses. Made such a pest of myself with all my questions that Josh finally hired me to shut me up. He figured a couple of days mucking out stalls and I'd conveniently forget to appear one morning."

"And?" Dane glanced over to encounter her velvet eyes watching his every move.

Robynn smiled at him, lazily, like they had all the time in the world and had known each other for centuries.

"And I never missed. The track became my second home; Josh, the grandfather I never knew."

"How do your parents feel about your racing?" Dane took a long swallow of his pop.

"At first they pitched a fit. Dad hollered and Mom cried. It didn't help. I inherited all their stubbornness combined. Now Mom figures I've worn out more than my contingent of guardian angels, but she loves to watch the ponies run. You'll see them nearly every weekend up in the stands. They're the two short, pudgy people, waving their programs and screaming, "That's our Robynn! Go get 'em, O'Dell!""

Dane laughed at the picture she created. "They sound like pretty special people."

"You turn here." Robynn pointed to the exit for northbound 205. "They are. They've always stood by me. Especially when . . ." Her smile flitted away like a dandelion puff blown by the breeze. The remembered agony doused the sparkle in her eyes. *You've got to tell him about Jeremy.* Her little voice was becoming persistent.

Dane waited for her to continue. When she didn't, he gently squeezed her hand, then released it to negotiate the curves taking them up onto the new freeway. Running straight again, he glanced back at her.

Robynn fought for control as the rough days crept back into her mind. The doctor's office had been decorated all in beiges and browns. The earth tones were supposed to be restful, but the antiseptic smell still made patients aware of their surroundings. The sleeping infant lay exhausted in her arms after all the tests. By the time the doctors were finished, he had arched his back and waved his tiny fists, a miniature prize-fighter taking on the world. His furious screams ricocheted off the walls.

His anger hadn't helped.

Nothing had helped. The verdict remained the same. Blind.

The doctors wanted to promise hope, but there was none. For some reason, Jeremy's eyes had never finished developing. What wasn't there couldn't be repaired.

Robynn might have gone under without God's presence in her life after Sonny's departure. While her cries of "Why God?" seemed to go spinning into the eternal black holes of space, the comfort promised in the Scriptures tiptoed in and wrapped her in the love and reassurance she needed for her baby. God's touch came to her in people: doctors, nurses, counselors, and the pastor and members of the church she had turned to.

Drifting away from that closeness had happened gradually as her busy life took over. While she tried to stifle such feelings, sometimes resentment of God's role or lack of it reared its ugly head. It was hard not to ask *Why me?*, not to blame God for both the death and the blindness.

But the counsel of the medical people, her friends, and family had been correct. Jeremy grew into a delightful little boy, learning to enjoy life in spite of his disability. Now he was getting the training needed to become an independent person. Training all the mother-love in the world couldn't give him.

Dane waited patiently for Robynn to come back from the far reaches of her mind. Gently, his thumb stroked the limp hand in his.

"Who is it that hurt you?" His soft voice helped Robynn slam the door on her memories.

"It couldn't be helped." She became aware of the warmth radiating from her enclosed hand and up her arm. It would be so easy to tell him everything. No man had ever created that desire in her before. She had always kept her feelings to herself. Her air of aloofness contributed to her nickname.

Robynn took a deep breath and tilted her chin a fraction higher. After a quick smile at the man beside her, she stared straight ahead. She would manage. She always had. Robynn O'Dell did not need the care and comforting of any man, especially this one. Good feelings sometimes became weak feelings, and she was not weak. Not by a long shot. Maybe that was why she had a hard time letting God in, too: She had such a driving need to do things herself. A Bible verse from her childhood echoed softly in her ears. *"I can do all things through Christ which strengthens me."*

She chuckled to herself. *I like the first part of that verse. The last half . . .*

"Can you let me in on the joke?"

She shrugged. *So where is he in matters of faith?* She knew she wouldn't make a mistake like Sonny again. But as Josh so often reminded her, she and Sonny had both been so young. Hardships had a way of making you grow up—fast. Grow better or bitter, that was always the choice, according to her dad.

Robynn glanced at the paper in her hand. "You turn to the right up there." She changed the subject. "From the looks of this address, this farm must be out by Opal's."

"Good. Maybe we can stop there, too. I can see the others on the list another time."

"You hadn't planned on looking at all of them today, had you?" Robynn stared at the list of addresses. "It'll be dark before long."

It didn't take them two minutes to look at the first farm. Dane didn't even get out of the car. One glance at the house, rundown barn, and swampy pastureland, and he reversed the Porsche. The powerful car threw gravel getting out the driveway.

"So much for the Realtor's description of 'slight fixer-upper.'" Dane snorted his contempt. "You'd think after the guidelines I gave, they'd know what I want. I was very explicit." Dane detailed again the requirements he had set up.

A pang shot through Robynn as she realized what a contrast Opal's farm would be to the one they'd just seen. She was almost tempted to bypass it and take the next one on the list.

"You said the McKecknen farm is near here?" Dane shot down her idea before it crystallized into action.

"Turn right, then left at the intersection." Mechanically Robynn gave the instructions.

"What's wrong?" Dane's puzzled look made her aware again how closely she must guard her thoughts. The man was so perceptive. *Wonder what it would be like to live with someone that sensitive?*

Get a hold of yourself, girl, her inner voice scolded her. *Remember, you said no men.*

"McKecknen's Racing Stable," Dane read the sign aloud. Even in the deepening dusk, the white board fences beckoned one up the drive. The welcoming arms of the U-shaped house at the top of the rise invited all comers to enter and make themselves at home. A wide doorway and smiling window eyes radiated warmth, much as their gracious owner did.

Dane remained silent as they slowly drove up the asphalt drive. Robynn watched him as his gaze took in everything. Only his hands tensing on the wheel betrayed any feelings.

She sensed his mental cash register tallying up the cost. Without a doubt, this place would be worth every penny Opal was asking.

"It's perfect," Dane finally said, with a sigh. "I feel like I've come home."

"You haven't seen the inside of the house or the barns or checked out the land or . . ." Robynn could feel herself babbling to distract him. He couldn't feel this was his home yet. She and Josh and Jeremy had to have first chance. She realized the car had been motionless for several minutes.

Turning, she found Dane regarding her with a question in his dark eyes. "You don't want me to have this farm, do you?" His tone was flat. More of a statement than a question. "Why?"

"What makes you think that?"

"Lady, you're as easy to read as a foal at feeding time."

"Would you like to see the barns?" Robynn interrupted. "Opal's car isn't here, so I don't think anyone is home. You'll have to tour the house another time." She unbuckled her seat belt and opened the door. When she hadn't heard any movement, she turned. Dane leaned against his door, staring at her. A slight frown drew his heavy black brows closer together.

Robynn discovered what a victim must feel like when mesmerized by a cobra. Dane seemed to be peeling layer after layer from her mind to get down to the core of her.

"If you'd rather not," she offered halfheartedly.

Without a word and without taking his eyes from her, Dane unsnapped his seat belt and opened the door. With a slight nod, he slid from behind the wheel and unfolded his broad frame to stand beside the vehicle.

When Robynn straightened outside the car, she found him leaning his elbows on the roof, all the while studying the lay of the land. Immaculate. A show place. Home. These were some of the words Robynn had heard used to describe this jewel of a ranch. To the east, the Cascades backdropped the rolling hills of the McKecknen place.

"On a clear day, you can see Mount St. Helens over there." She pointed at an impenetrable cloud bank toward the north. "And in the winter, even the foothills usually have snow on them. If that's important to you, that is."

"It is to you?" His soft question drew her eyes back to his. Gone was the stern face of a few moments ago. In its place was the caring look he'd worn in the car, when she'd disappeared into her memories.

"Yes." She turned and led the way up the gravel road to the stables.

The mercury yard lights cast a bright glow by the time Dane and Robynn finished their inspection of the outbuildings and the animals. Dane watched her surrounded by her inquisitive friends in the pasture. One of the colts nuzzled her pocket, obviously used to finding treats in it.

"You do more than just ride for Opal, don't you?" Dane asked as they climbed back in the car.

"Yes. I help break the two-year-olds and work with the other stock when I can." She buckled her seat belt by herself this time. "I love the foals. Did you see that black filly run? She's going to be something one of these days." Enthusiasm brought the sparkle back to her eyes. "And that bay mare? That's Finding Fun's dam. She's bred to—"

Dane chuckled as he started the engine. "Enough, woman." He shifted into reverse. The silver car spun in a tight circle, obedient to the strong hands on the wheel. "I'm starved. How about you?"

Robynn relaxed against the seat, grateful for the return of the feeling of camaraderie. The darkness cocooned them in the rich-smelling interior as the car picked up speed on the main road. Black asphalt sparkled diamonds in the headlights when a slight sprinkle dampened the road. Even the rhythmic swish and click of the wiper blades when the drizzle turned to rain added to Robynn's sense of well-being. On hold were the fears of losing the farm and animals. She was content to enjoy the moment.

"Do you know where you're going?" she finally asked.

"We're going."

"What?"

"Not just me. Wherever I go, you go, too. You see, you're in the same car as I and—"

"Dane!" She playfully pushed his arm. "I didn't ask for a lesson in semantics. A simple answer would suffice."

"Wait and see."

"Thanks a lot."

"You're welcome." At his polite nod, a duet of laughter sang counterpoint to the wiper blades.

When they finally drew up in front of a log building, Robynn looked around with interest. A wooden bridge arched over a low waterfall that joined two ponds. Underwater lights shimmered as the raindrops splashed on the surface, dripping like tears from the weeping willow overhanging the pond's edge.

"Dane, you utterly amaze me." Robynn shook her head in astonishment. "How'd you hear about this place? I've never been here before."

"Just asked about a good place for steaks and a rustic atmosphere." He came around the car to open her door. "At your service, ma'am." Robynn placed her hand in his to rise from the low seat.

They had finished ordering before Robynn had time to inspect their surroundings. Rounded knotty-pine half-logs finished the walls and the individual booths. Steins of every size and description paraded across the heavy plank mantel above a fieldstone fireplace, complete with roaring blaze.

Old-fashioned wagon wheel lights provided dim overhead illumination, while on each table small hurricane lamps flickered with any passing breath.

Dane reached across the table to cover her folded hands with his own. The sparks leaped back to life.

"You're really a special person." His words rumbled low in his throat. When he leaned forward, the lamplight cast shadows over his lean face, highlighting carved-granite cheekbones.

"Yours was the blue cheese, right, sir?" The waitress slid a chilled salad plate in front of him.

I'll come back to this later, his eyes silently promised Robynn before he smiled politely up at the cheery young woman. The fringe on the western suede vest and skirt flounced as she finished serving them.

"Can I get you anything else?" She paused.

"No. That's fine, thank you." Dane smiled in dismissal.

By the time they finished their perfectly done, charcoal-seared steaks, Robynn could feel her eyelids begin to droop. The combined effects of warm room and full stomach, plus a day that had begun at five in the morning, were wearing on her. With a sigh, she leaned back against the hard wood of the seat back.

"Tired?"

"Um. Beat. But that was a marvelous dinner."

"Dessert?"

"I'm a jockey, remember?"

"Don't remind me." Dane studied her across the table. "I think I better take you home."

Robynn only nodded.

The ride home passed quickly as the powerful machine ate up the miles. The roads were well marked, so Robynn didn't need to concentrate to give him directions. Instead, she rested her head against the soft leather seat and slipped into slumber, a soft smile curving her lips.

After he killed the engine in her driveway, Dane watched her for a moment before gently shaking her shoulder. "Hey, sleepyhead. You're home."

Her eyelids fluttered open. The curve of her lovely lips deepened. As her eyes met his, Dane leaned forward toward her. Slowly, tantalizingly, his lips brushed hers.

"Goodnight, Princess," he breathed against her cheek. "Thank you for a very special evening."

He jackknifed himself from the low-slung car and came around to help her out. Her arm tucked securely in his, they strolled up the walk to the back door. The tang hanging in the air from a neighbor's fireplace sharpened the evening air like a touch of tarragon in veal cordon bleu. At the bottom of the cement steps, Dane turned her to face him, clasping both her hands in his.

Robynn waited, savoring the anticipation. Their gazes locked.

"Goodnight, Princess," he whispered as he finally pulled away. "I'll see you tomorrow."

Bemused, Robynn slid her key in the lock and opened her door. Reluctant to lose her rosy glow, she bypassed the light switch, making her way to the bedroom in the soft reflection from the street lamps.

A red flashing signal on her answering machine caught her attention.

She flicked the play switch while she hung her coat in the closet.

"This is Emmanuel Hospital. We admitted Josh MacDonald at nine-thirty this evening. He asked us to notify you. He'll be going into surgery shortly."

The hanger banged against the bar as Robynn ripped her coat back out of the closet and shoved her arms in the sleeves on her mad dash to the car.

FIVE

Oh, God, no. Not Josh." She slammed the door behind her. "Please, let him be all right. Make him all right. Please." *Please* was the litany her mind sang as she clashed out to the garage. Within seconds her black Celica roared out into the street. Impatiently, she stopped at the lights; every one seemed to turn red as she approached. As the caution yellow appeared for the traffic coming the opposite way, she gunned the motor, the car pushing against the brake like an impatient Thoroughbred at the starting gate.

She started to release the avid machine when she heard the roar of an approaching vehicle and slammed her foot on the brake. The Celica stalled partway into the intersection. With a cheery wave, the driver of a red Corvette saluted her quick reflexes. His blinking taillights mocked her shaking hands and pounding heart.

Robynn checked both ways before she turned the key to bring the engine back to life again. Biting her lip to stop its quivering, she drove the remaining distance at a Sunday driver's pace.

"Well, my girl," she reminded herself, "you wouldn't have been much help being wheeled into the emergency room on a gurney yourself."

What right do you have asking for favors and care? the guilt side of her brain questioned. *You haven't been worshiping or reading your Bible or . . . in fact, the only time you think about God is when you need something. What kind of a relationship is that?*

But—

She turned off any excuses, telling herself she'd deal with this later.

With a sigh, Robynn acknowledged the warring factions in her mind. Swiftly she locked the door and, stuffing the key in its outside pocket, swung her shoulder bag in place. Her boots beat a double-time tattoo as she entered the hospital, the swoosh of the automatic door the only greeting.

The woman at the main desk finished a ledger entry before she looked up. "May I help you?" Her face looked as if a smile might crack it, shattering the rigid lines into slivers.

"Uh, someone here called. I'm Robynn O'Dell to see Josh MacDonald. I understand he's been in an accident."

With all the speed of a sedentary slug, the woman sorted through her notes. "Yes. Here it is." She removed her half glasses. "Go on up to five. There's a waiting room right by the elevators."

"Can I see him?"

The woman meticulously placed her glasses back on her patrician nose and consulted her notes. "You can ask at the desk up there. They'll know more than I do." The eyes peering over the flat frames of the horn-rimmed glasses might have been chipped from a glacier.

"Thank you."

The woman almost nodded as she traced back to her place in the ledger.

Robynn strode impatiently to the bank of elevators down the hall. *That woman must be a real comfort to people who come here,* she thought as she punched the up button.

"Dr. Davis to pediatrics," the intercom echoed as she entered the metal box. "Dr. Davis to pediatrics."

Alone in the rising elevator, Robynn stared at the signs for no smoking and load limits without consciously seeing them. She gnawed her bottom lip, willing the silent elevator to hurry, willing Josh to respond, to be all right.

The strong smell of antiseptic penetrated her concentration as she stepped into the night-dimmed hall. Somewhere down the hall, a weak voice cried, "Help me. Someone please help me?"

Robynn shuddered.

The lights created a comforting oasis at the nurses' counter. The young nurse working on reports at the lower desk looked up immediately as Robynn approached the high shelf. "Hi," she said with a smile. "What can I do for you?"

"It's about Josh MacDonald. I received word on my answering machine that he's been hurt. The receptionist said to come up here."

While Robynn talked, the nurse quickly scanned her lists. "Yes, he's in the recovery room now. They should be bringing him to his room in about half an hour."

"Er-r, can you tell me, do you know what happened?"

"I'm sorry." The voice sounded really apologetic. "I don't know any details. If you'll wait in that room over there," she pointed to a pair of swinging doors, "the doctor can tell you when he comes out."

"Thanks." Robynn turned to follow directions. "Oh." She spun on her heel. "Where can I find a phone?"

"Is it a local call?"

"Um-hmm." Robynn nodded.

"Here, you can use this one. Just don't tell anyone." The nurse winked at her.

Robynn thanked her and dialed Josh's home number. Surely Dane had made it back by this time. She glanced at her watch. It must have been half an hour since she'd heard the messages on her machine.

"Dane, this is Robynn," she announced as a groggy voice finally answered the ringing phone. "I'm at Emmanuel Hospital. Josh has been in an accident."

"How bad is it?" His voice immediately snapped with authority.

"I don't know. I haven't seen the doctor and Josh is still in recovery."

"There was surgery then?"

"Um-hmm."

"I'll be there as quick as I can. Where is it?"

"Go south on I-5. You'll see the hospital off to the left. Take the next exit." Robynn's memory flashed back to her near miss. "Drive carefully."

The empty line buzzed in her ear. When Dane went into action, he didn't waste time. Robynn smiled her thanks at the nurse as she hung up the phone. Her booted heels tapped overloud in the nighttime hush of the darkened hall. As she passed an open door, someone groaned. Robynn stepped up her pace but tried to walk more on her toes. The hovering miasma of pain and agony called for a silent passage.

In the waiting room, she tried to relax on the rigid couch but found herself looking up at every sound, hoping one would be the doctor coming out. The double swinging beige doors leading to the surgical wing had big signs: "NO ADMITTANCE."

She heard rapid footsteps coming down the hall at the same moment the doors opened. A tired-looking man in green cotton surgical garb wiped a weary hand across his forehead and removed the green mask that dangled from its strings.

"Are you Robynn O'Dell?"

Robynn nodded. At the same moment, she felt her hand taken by a larger one.

"I'm Dane Morgan, Doctor. Josh's nephew. What can you tell us?"

"He has numerous superficial lacerations and contusions. But the real problem is his right leg. The force of the impact shattered the tibia. I've had to pin it, and he'll be in traction for a time."

"But he'll be all right?" Robynn asked.

"Yes, barring complications."

"What happened?" Dane questioned.

"He was brought in from an automobile accident, furious at the idiot who ran the red light. I have the feeling," the doctor smiled at them, "he's not going to be a very good patient. First thing out of the anesthetic, he demanded crutches and a walking cast. Says he has horses to race."

"When can we see him?"

"They're bringing him to Room 515 now. He'll be pretty groggy for a while, but you can talk to him if you want."

"Thank you, sir." Robynn extended her hand. "I appreciate all you've done."

"You're Robynn O'Dell, the jockey, aren't you?" the doctor asked as they turned to leave.

"Yes, I am. Why?"

"My friend, Dr. Benson, raves about what a great rider you are. He's trying to talk me into going partners with him on a horse."

"You'd enjoy it. Thanks again." Robynn felt her feet flying down the hall as Dane hurried her with a strong hand under her elbow.

As they opened the door, the nurse was just finishing adjusting the weights and pulley contraption attached to a heavy cast. Only the tense white lines around Josh's mouth spoke of the pain he suffered. One eye was swollen shut, but the other blinked open instantly when Robynn whispered his name.

"Took you long enough to get here." Josh's voice belied the weakened state of his body.

"And a thank you for coming to you, too." Robynn grinned in relief at his ill humor. "I can see you have been knocked down but not out."

"What time is it?" Josh turned his head, looking for a clock.

"Midnight." Dane checked his watch. "For whatever difference that makes."

"Fool driver hit me on my way home from the track. About nine. I've got so much to do, and now that fool doctor says I'll be laid up for weeks." Pain closed his good eye for a moment when he moved more than his head.

"It'll be okay, Josh." Robynn stroked the gnarled hand lying on the white bedspread. "I know what needs to be done. I'll manage."

"No. You can't handle it all." He struggled to move his tousled head. "Dane. You're going to have to take over for me at the track. You know the procedures. They're not any different than those down south. Robynn here'll introduce you to all the people you need to know."

"But Josh." A note of pleading crept into her voice.

"I can handle it." Dane stepped closer to the bed.

She flashed a glance of resentment at the tall man by her side.

"And Dane," Josh raised his hand long enough for Dane to take it. "No matter what your personal beliefs, Robynn races. She's the only jockey who's ever been up on most of those animals. They go best for her."

Now it was Dane's turn to narrow his eyes and tighten his jawline. The moment stretched.

"They're not your horses—yet." The old man closed his good eye and his hand dropped back to the bed. "And now, off with both of ye. You'll be needing your sleep."

Robynn leaned over and kissed the wrinkled cheek. Josh looked twenty years older than he had that afternoon. "Talk to you tomorrow," she whispered.

"Let me know how you do."

"Yes." She turned at the door, but Dane's tall body blocked her view. When she raised her gaze to his, ice sheathed the blue depths.

"Why are you mad at me?" She asked when they entered the down elevator.

"I don't want you racing."

"It doesn't matter what you want."

"It does when I'm in charge of the horses. And giving the jockey orders." He crossed his arms over his chest.

"Well, you heard Josh."

"Yes. But I don't have to like it." Again a hand under her arm propelled her along after they reached the lobby.

Stung by his reply, Robynn seethed all the way to the cars, trying to think of some appropriately scathing reply. None came.

"Well, then." After climbing in her car, she smiled up at him so sweetly the honey dripped from each syllable. "We'll just have to agree to disagree, won't we?"

The slam of his car door was her only answer.

Robynn's alarm buzzed before she'd even had time to roll over during the short night. Groggy, with sleep still locking her eyelashes together, she staggered into the bathroom and a hot shower. When even the stinging water couldn't force her eyes open, she turned on the cold. With a yelp, she was wide awake and reaching for the towel.

Dawn still snoozed when she swung her car into the rain-drenched parking lot. The drizzle let up to a light mist as she dogtrotted through the gate and to the barns.

Dane already had grain in front of all the horses as though used to the familiar routine.

"Didn't you go home at all?" Robynn asked when she found him in the far stall checking out the horses scheduled for racing in the afternoon.

"Of course I did." He straightened from picking the horse's hooves. "What took you so long?" The cheery note in his voice took the sting out of the words.

"Actually, I'm early. He okay?" She nodded at the huge bay calmly munching his grain.

"Sure. How about taking Finding Fun out first? She's a fast eater, just needs to be loosened up."

"Fine." Robynn stared out at the drops splashing over the eaves. "Sure wish this rain would let up. You'd think it was the middle of January or something." She followed him as he entered the next stall. "Watch this one. He bi—"

"Ouch! You stupid . . ." Dane jerked the halter of the dark gelding. "Knock it off!" The horse turned back to his manger. He'd made his point.

"Here, you hold his head." Dane turned to glare at her. Robynn could hardly hide the giggles threatening to erupt. Dane caught the laughter in her eyes. "You could have warned me sooner." He rubbed his shoulder. "At least he bites rather gently."

"Yeah, he just likes to show any new man who's boss. He's never bitten me." Robynn rubbed the tender spot up behind the horse's ears. The munch of grain and the drip of the incessant rain were the only sounds as Dane stroked down each leg, searching for hot spots and swelling.

He's thorough, that's for sure, Robynn thought as she watched him calmly go about his business. *If only he didn't have such a thing about female jockeys. For such a smart man, how can he be so stupid?*

By the time dawn had lightened the sky to dull gray, Robynn had already had three horses out. The rapport between her and Dane settled into any easy working relation-ship, each aware of the expertise of the other. Dane boosted her up each time, then watched the workouts from the covered bleachers.

Once mounted on the fourth, Robynn settled herself and stroked the sleek neck of the waiting animal. Come Runnin' reached around to sniff her boot.

"Yeah, it's me." She smoothed his mane. "Did you think we were gonna pull a switch on you?" Robynn laughed at the question in Dane's eyes. "I'm the only one who's ever ridden him. I broke him last year and raced him toward the end of the season as a two-year-old." She leaned forward to pull some hair from under the headstall. "Weren't quite grown up yet, were you old man?" She rubbed just behind his ears. Come Runnin' sighed.

"We didn't do too well," Robynn shook her head. "He was like a young teenager in the worst of the growing stages. Clumsy and just not ready." Awareness of the depth of blue in Dane's eyes penetrated her monologue. "He ah–m . . ."

My goodness, her mind filled in the gaps, *but he's a handsome hunk of man. Why'd he have to come into my life just now? I don't have time for any more complications. And I think he's going to make things really complicated.*

"He what?" Dane prompted her, stroking the horse's shoulder.

"Well, he wasn't ornery or anything, but not placid like he is now, either."

"What happened?"

Robynn shrugged her shoulders. "Well, we took a bit of a tumble one day."

"In a race?"

Robynn lifted her reins. "We better get going. I've got a lot to do."

Dane rubbed the horse's ears in the same place Robynn had. Come Runnin' leaned against him, grateful for the attention.

"Robynn, was the fall during a race?" He emphasized each word, his diction clipping the sounds. His smile had been tucked away, back where Robynn couldn't even see a glimmer.

Why'd you let yourself in for this? she scolded herself. *You knew how he felt. Get a grip, girl.*

"Dane, no one got hurt . . ."

"That's not what I asked." A tiny muscle worked at the side of his mouth. "Was it during a race?"

"Yes! And don't say 'I told you so.' Falls sometimes go with the territory. It wasn't anyone's fault, and besides that I've learned how to fall. I'm a jockey and a good one." The tension from her voice and mind crept to her knees. Come Runnin' sidestepped and gazed longingly at the track. He pulled at the restraining hand on his bridle.

Robynn shivered as she felt the mist creeping into her bones. She pulled her goggles down and settled them in place. "Remember," she turned the horse toward the track and spoke over her shoulder, "we agreed to disagree." Come Runnin' broke into a trot at the pressure of her calves. As he cleared the gate he pulled at the bit, begging to run.

"Tomorrow you get to run, fella." Her voice fell into its easy singsong. It worked. Horses always responded to her voice and calm hands. Even the most fractious settled down. "That's one of the things that makes me a good jockey," she sang to the long pointed ears that kept turning back to listen to her, then forward to catch the sounds from in front. "And I *am* a good jockey. Someday, I'll be one of the best. One of these days there'll be another O'Dell, top jock at Portland Meadows. And besides, I need the money."

Come Runnin' settled into the easy lope that ate up the miles and hardly raised a sweat. As they passed other horses, he worked the snaffle bit with his tongue, like a little kid begging for a cookie. At her insistence he relaxed but kept the same pace.

"If all my mounts were as easy as you." Robynn eased him back to a trot.

Two horses later, while Dane clipped the cross tie ropes onto a steaming horse, Robynn pulled the gloves from her freezing fingers. She tucked her hands under her armpits and jogged in place to get some feeling back in her feet.

"Cruddy weather!" she muttered to herself, low so Dane couldn't hear her.

As Robynn circled the track with her last mount, the breeze shifted to a bone-chilling wind from the east. Blowing down the Columbia Gorge, the cold weather hit the racetrack full strength. The drizzle flattened into a driving rain that plastered Robynn's down jacket to her back. One by one, the horses left the track.

When Robynn trotted her mount up to the stalls, Dane appeared out of the downpour to lift her down. "Thanks," she shivered the word out.

"Do you have dry clothes here?" He might have been speaking to a three-year-old.

Robynn was too cold to argue. "Y-y-es-s-s."

"I'll go call Josh and meet you for breakfast in half an hour. A long shower ought to warm you up."

Robynn grabbed her duffel bag from the tack room and trotted across the road to the dressing rooms.

"Hey, Princess, you look about froze clear through," Pam Highden, Robynn's best friend, called. "Didn't you have sense enough to quit?"

"Wanted to get done first."

"How's Josh?"

"He'll be laid up for a while. But he's tough."

Amazed at the speed of the track info line, Robynn dropped her soaked jacket on the bench. The bootjack made short work of her tall black boots as she pulled an old woolen sweater over her head. By the time her white turtle-neck joined the pile of clothes, the warmth of the room had begun to penetrate. The goose bumps on her skin receded to mosquito bite size.

"Hey." Pam dug through her duffle. "You got any shampoo?" Robynn tossed her the plastic bottle.

"Do you ever forget anything?" Pam asked as they entered the showers.

"Yeah, I'm bad on birthdays and anniversaries. Except for Jeremy's." Robynn turned the shower to full force. Steam billowed, speeding the defrosting process, starting from the toes up.

"How's Jeremy doing?" Pam shouted above the thundering water.

"Fine. He likes the school now." Robynn turned and let the hot fingers of water massage her back. "Has a super housemother. Mrs. Cravens. Really a neat grandmother-type person."

"Sounds good."

"Yeah. Tomorrow's my day to visit."

"Speaking of visits . . ." Pam peeked around the shower stall. "Who was that hunk I saw you with this morning? Been holding out on me?"

"I just met him the other day."

"Didn't look that way to me. Or you got friendly mighty fast."

"Well, you know how fast us jockeys are."

"Oh sure. Robynn O'Dell, the untouchable Princess. The only time you're fast is on the homestretch with a horse under you." Pam wrapped a towel around her bony figure. "You haven't even looked at anyone since Sonny, no matter how many great men I've introduced you to. The 'Ice Princess,' that's what some of the guys call you."

"Hey, that's not fair. I'm friendly to everyone."

"Not the kind of friendly they want. But . . . you looked pretty friendly with whatever-his-name-is."

"It's Dane Morgan." Robynn shut off the shower, wrapped the emerald green towel around her, and tucked in the ends. "He's Josh's nephew from California, looking for some horses and a farm."

"Wheee. Must be loaded. And good lookin', too." Pam rolled her hazel eyes toward the ceiling. "A winning combination." They collected their supplies and headed back to their clothes. "Is he married?"

Robynn stared at her, confusion stamped all over her expressive face.

Pam snorted. "You don't know, do you?"

Robynn shook her head. "He doesn't act married."

"Them's the worst kind, babe. Before you go losing your heart over him, you find out."

"But . . ."

"No buts, Princess." Pam snapped her skintight jeans. "Men play by different rules."

"What am I supposed to do? Walk up to him and say, 'Dane, are you married?'" Robynn slammed her feet into her ankle-high boots.

"I'm just warning you. You've been hurt enough already." Pam plugged in her blow dryer. "Yeah, I know." Pam made a face. "I'm bossy, nosey, and . . ."

"And a good friend." Robynn applied black mascara to her lashes.

"Thanks. But you *will* be careful?"

Robynn nodded at the concerned face in the mirror.

Careful, she thought. *That's what I've been for years and now . . .* She stuffed her hairbrush and toiletries back into her duffel bag.

"You ready to eat?" Robynn slung the bag over her shoulder.

"Yeah, but I'll be a few more minutes. You go ahead. Hey!" Pam called as Robynn opened the door. "You might save me a place at your table so I can meet him."

Robynn only had to step into the cafeteria when her "Dane Morgan interception system" picked up his signals. Dane lifted a beckoning hand as her eyes zeroed in on his. Robynn waved back, feeling like the sun had just peeked through the leaden skies.

By the time she had loaded her tray and approached the table, Dane and another trainer were deep in a discussion about training Thoroughbreds. Dane stood and pulled out the chair next to him, a smile brightening his face.

Robynn removed her dishes from the tray and slid it onto the table behind them. She tried to concentrate on her food, but her eyes tracked back to Dane's face, waiting for the warm smiles he seemed unable to suppress whenever he glanced at her.

"What do you think?" Dane snapped his fingers in front of her eyes. "Robynn, come back. I asked you a question."

"Um-m-m." She blinked. "I must have been daydreaming. What did you want?"

"You looked to be enjoying yourself. You were smiling, at least." Dane teased her. "I asked when you were going up to the hospital. And do you think Josh will be ready for company from some of his friends here? They've been asking."

"He'd love company, if I know him." Robynn smiled at the trainers and grooms gathered around them. Where had they all come from? Had she been that caught up in her daydreaming? "I'm going up before the afternoon program. I'm sure he's already champing at the bit."

The sound of a throat being cleared swung Robynn's attention to the slender woman standing next to her, her tray balanced on the back of a chair.

"Hey, you finally made it." Robynn indicated the chair. "Sit yourself."

When Dane stood to scoot in the chair, the other men nodded and went about their business.

"Pam Highden, this is Dane Morgan," Robynn made the introductions. "Dane is Opal's fill-in trainer."

"Trainer!" Pam sputtered. "But I thought..." She stared from Dane to Robynn. "Princess, you said..."

Dane looked at Robynn, expecting a response to the questions floating around, unasked and unanswered.

"Okay." Pam put on her no-nonsense voice. "What's going on here? In the first place, Dane, I'm glad to meet you." She stuck out her hand. "In the second place, what in the Sam Hill do they mean by trainer? Robynn said...ow–w–w!"

Robynn's booted toe, placed with force against Pam's shin, found its mark.

"What were you saying?" Robynn asked sweetly, her boot ready if another nudge was needed. "You don't think Dane will make a good trainer?"

"I think I better eat and keep my mouth shut." Pam dug into her grapefruit. "Don't mind me, folks."

Dane dropped his napkin on the table and scraped back his chair. "It was nice meeting you, Pam." He nodded in her direction. "But I've got to get back to the barns. Maybe you should spend the afternoon with Josh, Robynn. I can get someone else to ride for me today."

"Fat chance!" A frown settled on Robynn's brow. "I'll be back in plenty of time. And Dane." He turned back at her tone. "*I* ride the McKecknen horses. And any others my agent puts me on."

Dane touched his fingers to the brim of his felt hat, then strode out the doors.

Was that a defeat or victory? Robynn asked herself as she stared after him.

"Wow!" Pam tapped Robynn on the arm. "He's one gorgeous creature. Gives me the chills just looking at him."

"That's not what he gives me," Robynn grumbled.

"What's that all about?" Pam asked. "Getting someone to sub for you?"

"No, not sub. He doesn't want women jockeys in the races. A slightly antiquated opinion, but one he's dead set on."

"Why does anyone who looks so good have to be so bullheaded?" Pam moaned. "And after all the work we've done to get some equality out here. What are you going to do?"

"Ride the same as usual. Josh made him promise last night. But it looks like the man won't give up without a struggle."

"How many rides you got this afternoon?" Pam spread strawberry jam on her toast. "If we don't get rained out."

"No chance, the track's not running rivers yet. But it'll be slow going and slippery. Glad I'm only up twice, once for Josh on Jim Dandy, who hates the rain. And a mudder for Dr. Benson. Got a good chance on that one."

"They scratched mine for today. Doesn't break my heart any. I hate the wet worse'n your horse does. Maybe I'll head for sunny southern California when the season starts down there. Warm breezes, waving palm trees, blue sky, sunglasses instead of slickers." She sighed a deep sigh that echoed one of Robynn's.

Robynn drew up with a start when she realized her sunny daydream included a certain tall, dark, and forceful horse owner, now trainer. "Better get going." She slung her green raincoat around her shoulders. "Josh'll be as impatient as a nag at the feed trough to hear how the morning went."

At least Dane and I are still speaking, Robynn thought as she zipped her jacket against the chill. *Even if we don't like some of the stuff we're saying. Wonder what he's going to do next?*

SIX

$\mathcal{H}$i, Josh."

Robynn pushed open the hospital room door and entered his room. Banks of flowers and a fruit basket filled every spare counter, the window ledge, and part of the floor. "What have you done? Traded racing in for the florist's business?" She bent her head to inhale the fragrance of an arrangement of American Beauty roses.

"How'd you two do this morning?" Josh was not to be deflected from his main point.

"Fine. Didn't Dane call you?

"That he did, but I wanted to hear it from you as well. Last night I was afraid you might come to blows in the parking lot. Neither one of you hide your emotions very well."

Robynn leaned over to plant a kiss on his weathered cheek. "Give us some points for civility. This morning we were all sweetness and light." As she studied him, she could see the swelling had gone down in his eye. But both eyes had the slackness pain killers give. "Do you hurt bad?"

"No. They've got me so doped up all I do is sleep."

"Well, that's good. That way you're not jawing at them to let you up."

"It was miserable out there this morning, wasn't it?"

"Yeah. But we got through. They haven't canceled the program for this afternoon. Dane invited me to stay here with you. Said he'd get a sub."

"Determined, ain't he?"

"Um—m—m." Robynn read one of the cards on the flowers. "But then, so am I."

Josh nodded. "Called Opal this morning. She'll be here to meet with us at seven, okay?"

Robynn mentally checked her calendar. "That'll be fine. Thanks, Josh. I was afraid you'd forget."

"It's my leg that's busted, not my brain. Besides, lying here gives me all kinds of time to think ... too much time."

The two discussed the morning workout and planned strategies for the afternoon before Josh's eyes began to droop.

"I'll see you later," Robynn whispered.

Josh nodded. He forced his eyes open. "You be careful now, you hear?"

Robynn blew him a kiss from the door.

"Now be careful."

"I will, sir." Robynn nodded at the rounded man standing at her stirrups. His usually beaming face was creased with worry.

"Fools should have canceled the program. Maybe I'm the fool for letting you run."

"Not to worry. This is his kind of day." She stroked the mahogany shoulder of the horse under her. "You like the mud, don't you, fella?" Black ears twitched back and forth to listen to her.

"Well, you know him better'n I do, but ..."

"See you in the winner's circle."

Dr. Benson tried to smile at her confidence, but worry clouded his gray eyes. "You just be careful." He tapped her knee with each word. "Hear me?"

As the string of horses paraded to the post, Robynn hunched her shoulders. Even so, the drizzle discovered a crack between her helmet and silks and dripped down her neck. Peevish gusts of wind blew sheets of rain across the infield like silver curtains billowing in the breeze.

The start was slow, and the slogging mud kept the pace ponderous. Robynn's mount broke free by the second furlong and ran easily ahead of the pack, head up, enjoying the scenery. As they rounded the far turn, Robynn heard someone making a bid to catch them.

She leaned forward. "Come on, old man," she called to the twitching ears. "Let's go." He leveled out some more and crossed the wire ahead by two lengths.

"Just out for a Sunday drive, weren't you," Robynn laughed as she pulled the tall bay horse down to a trot to return to the winner's circle. He snorted and tossed his head, ready to go some more.

"See? What'd I tell you?" Robynn shook the good doctor's hand. His face was now wreathed with good cheer, belying his former concern.

"He looked like he was playing out there."

"Well, we had a good time, didn't we, fella?" Robynn scratched behind the twitching ears. The colt rubbed his muddy nose on her shoulder just as the flashbulbs clicked. Robynn grinned at all the good wishes.

"Congratulations." Dane's clipped voice and glowering expression made a lie out of his words. He took the reins and trotted off, leading the obedient animal.

Robynn shook her head as she stepped on the scale. Winning races was certainly going to be easier than winning him. Winning him? She started in surprise. Who said anything about even wanting him?

You did, the little voice inside teased her. *Think about your reactions to him. Winning with him sure is better than winning over him. Together, you two make quite a pair. Love never comes easy, you know.*

The rest of the afternoon passed in a shower of mud. Her agent had gotten her three new mounts, so Robynn was in the saddle most of the time and in the money every race she rode. The amount of her winnings kept pace with the adrenaline pumping through her system as she saw her bank account grow at each win and bring her a tiny mark closer to the reality of owning her own horses.

But exhaustion painted purple shadows under her eyes as the adrenaline dissipated after the last race. Even a shower failed to revive her. She slogged through the puddles out to her car, too weary to walk across the infield to the barns, so she drove around to the back gate.

Robynn pasted a smile on her face and forced her shoulders straight as she stepped into the stall where Dane squatted down, wrapping a horse's leg. With deft hands, he wound the bandages around the hot leg, being careful to keep them from cutting off the circulation. Even though he glanced up to see who was there, Dane began on the other foreleg without a word.

"How bad is he?" Robynn kept her voice noncommittal.

When Dane didn't answer, Robynn leaned against the wall. She closed her eyes and savored the smell of good hay, warm horseflesh, and the bite of liniment. Her green shiny jacket was the only spot of color in the dimly lit stall.

"That's all for you, boy." She heard Dane slap the blood bay horse's rump. Robynn opened her eyes to find him glaring down at her.

"You're so tired you're asleep on you feet."

"Ah. But thousands of dollars richer." Robynn knew her flippant answer was a mistake before it was out of her mouth. Dane slammed a fist against the wall above her head.

"You're nothing but a money hungry . . ."

"Say it," Robynn flared back at him. "Money isn't important until you don't have enough."

"But you're taking your life in your hands." He reached for her waist. "I saw you nearly go down out there. Is money worth that?"

"Maybe what money can buy is." She twisted away from him. "And who made you my keeper? I've been racing for a long time without your smothering."

Dane glared down at her. The silence stretched until the curious horse nudged him in the back. "We'll discuss this later," he snapped. "I have work to do."

"What do you want me to do?"

"Nothing. Get out of here and go home to get some sleep. I'll pick you up for dinner at seven."

"No you won't." Robynn stared at him, appalled at his ordering her around. "I already have something I have to do."

"Fine. I'll help you." He walked off as if the conversation were finished.

Robynn trotted to catch up with him. When he didn't stop, she grabbed his arm. "Dane Morgan. You don't understand. I don't want to discuss my racing with you. I don't want to go home to bed. And most of all, I don't want to have dinner with you tonight."

Dane leaned back against the barn, arms crossed over his chest. "Anything else?"

"No."

"I'll see you at seven." A twinkle peeked out of his eyes, as though testing to see if the climate were right. He uncrossed his arms and, reaching out one tanned forefinger, brushed the wavy hair back off her cheek.

Robynn forced the frown to remain in place. "Dane!" Tiny electric pulses spread from the point of contact, darting up to smooth out her brow. She sighed as if she'd been holding her breath for a long time. "I won't be there," she whispered.

"Then I'll come and find you." He grasped her by the shoulders, turned her, and gently pushed her toward the exit. "See you."

Not if I see you first, Robynn fumed to herself. She was even more disgruntled to find herself doing exactly as he said. Bed did sound good.

Several hours later when she woke up, Robynn wasn't sure if she'd engaged in a shouting match with an icy-eyed Irishman or just dreamed it. The impression was so strong she found herself muttering as she pulled her clothes back on.

"I *will* keep racing. Not him, not accidents, nothing is going to stop me. After wins like today, that top jockey spot is coming closer. This year I may make it." She glared at her reflection in the mirror. "So there."

The woman at the desk hadn't thawed any when Robynn entered the hospital just before seven. She'd grabbed a hamburger on the way to make sure she was out of the house when Dane arrived. She refused to analyze her motives. Orders always made her feel rebellious.

As she entered the room, she saw a diminutive, gray-haired lady perched on the edge of the visitor's chair. She and Josh were talking a mile a minute. Hesitant to interrupt, Robynn paused in the door. If possible, there were more flowers in the room than had been that morning. The pervasive aroma completely blanketed the hospital odor.

"Hi, Princess." Josh raised a hand in greeting when he finally noticed her. "You'll have to find another chair. They keep taking them out, hoping it will discourage visitors, I think."

"I take it there've been a few." Robynn gestured around at the colorful display.

"Yeah." Josh grinned. "One or two. I think some of them just needed a place out of the rain for a while."

"Josh MacDonald. You old rascal." Opal chided him. "You know better than that."

"That's right, let him have it." Robynn enjoyed the repartee between the two old friends. "How are you, Opal? Were you at the track today?"

"Of course. You rode well." Opal's precise diction harked back to her years of teaching English and speech. "I never dreamed Jim Dandy would run that well, in the mud especially."

"He's a fine colt." Robynn nodded. "You'll see him in the winner's circle more and more."

"That's what we need to talk about." Opal leaned forward. "I'm leaving next week for Phoenix. My daughter is ill. She needs me, and this is a perfect time to make the move. I've been planning it for some time. Her illness is just the catalyst."

"And . . ."

"And I want to sell the horses and the farm. You already knew that."

"Yes."

"Josh says the two of you would like a chance to purchase the animals, especially the racing stock."

"Um-m-m."

"I need a quarter million for the racing string. I haven't decided how much for the brood mares and colts. The farm is listed at $750,000. I've priced everything for a quick sale."

Robynn felt like someone had just socked her in the solar plexus. It was hard to breathe around the knot of muscles in her midriff. A quarter million! And that's just for the . . .

"I have appointments with several prospective buyers," Opal continued, "but I wanted to give you," she nodded at both of them, "the first chance."

"Would we be able to set up a contract?" Josh locked his hands behind his head. "Over a couple of years maybe?"

"The best terms I can give are seventy-five percent down and a year to pay it off. I'm sorry." She shrugged. "But I really need the money."

"When will you decide how much for the breeding stock?" Robynn asked. "Don't you have part ownership in that stud, too?"

"The other owners have already bought me out, and in answer to your first question, I'll know within the next two days."

Boy, you don't waste any time, Robynn thought. *A quarter million. Why, most people never see that amount of money all at one time in their entire life. And what about the mares? The foals? I want all of them. They're just like my kids.*

When she sells the place, there won't be any more farm for Jeremy. Where else could he ride and run and . . . why it'll be like losing a grandma for her to go.

Robynn settled back in her chair, slipping down so she rested on her tailbone. One finger tapped the wooden arm of the chair. None of her actions calmed the swirling in her mind.

"I can tell this has taken you by surprise." Opal leaned forward in her chair. "I really hadn't planned to be so abrupt, but then I didn't know how much money we would need for my daughter's treatment."

"That's an understatement if I ever heard one." Robynn shook her head. "I feel knocked down and run over. Guess I just never totaled it up before. But I sure do understand about needing money to help your daughter."

"Can we ask a favor?" Josh lowered his gaze from contemplating the acoustical tile.

"Of course."

"Can you give us until tomorrow to think about, discuss this?"

"Tomorrow I go to see Jeremy . . ."

"How about until Friday?" Opal interrupted. "You need to go on your visit." She nodded at Robynn. "That should give you some business hours to find backing. How does that sound?"

"You won't take any offers in the meantime?" Josh punctuated the statement with his hand.

"No. Everything will be on hold. I'll meet my appointments, but no money will change hands until I talk with you." Opal picked up her leather purse from the floor and stood. "Now, Josh, you behave yourself so you can get out of here more quickly." She patted his hand.

"See you later." Robynn smiled but remained where she was while Opal strode briskly out of the room. With a heavy sigh, Josh sank back against his pillows.

"Well, now we know." He stared glumly at the roses amassed by the sink.

"Yeah."

"You'll talk to your parents?"

"Um. Tonight I guess. It's about time I visited them anyway. Glad Dad wasn't there today. He's a worse fussbudget than Dane."

"You given any thought to why he acts the way he does?"

"Who? Dad or Dane?"

"Either one. Both. I think the reason is the same."

"What are you talking about?"

"It's all a matter of caring."

"Josh, in case it's slipped your mind, I met Dane Morgan only the other day. It's hardly fair to compare him to my father. I've known *him* slightly longer than forty-eight, no seventy-two hours."

Ignoring her sarcasm, Josh stared into her eyes.

The moment stretched.

"Josh!"

"I'm just calling 'em as I see 'em."

Like a frisky colt on a summer's day, Robynn's mind darted back to each of the encounters with Dane. They got along just great, in fact better than great, she admitted as she thought of the kiss in the Porsche. That is, until the discussion got around to her racing. In reality, no man she'd ever met sent awareness racing up and out her nerves like he did.

"But I've no more chances of getting hurt than the next guy. He's just a chauvinist, thinks women'll go to pieces in a race."

"Maybe *your* being beat to pieces under some horse is the problem."

"I think it's stupid that he worries about me." Robynn slammed her palm on the chair arm and shoved the chair back. "And you can just tell him so."

"Tell who what?" A deep voice sent the aforethought of tingles back out where they made her fingers and toes feel alive again.

"Tell him yourself." Josh fumbled for the call button pinned to the edge of his bed. "I'll talk to the nurse."

Before the silence had stretched to an uncomfortable degree, the cheery nurse bustled into the room. Dane and Robynn rose and walked out the door as she whipped the sliding curtain around the bed.

"Would you like to go out to the waiting room and sit down?"

"Not particularly." His hand on her arm sent signals over her body again.

"You weren't at the house."

"Very perceptive of you."

"Are you running away from me?" He turned so she had to look at him or stare at the floor.

"I wasn't the one giving the orders."

"Is it wrong to want to take care of you?" He crossed his arms over his chest.

"What gives you the idea that I need caring for? I've managed my life pretty well up to now." Her renegade mind flashed back to the comfort, the warmth she found in his arms. "And I intend to continue the same way. I don't need you or anyone else messing me up."

"Is that what I do? Mess you up?"

Startled, Robynn stared at him. A five o'clock shadow deepened the cleft in his chin, causing his eyes to seem even bluer and his hair blacker. The force in his gaze willed her to answer.

"I think I hear my mother calling," she whispered.

Dane stared back at her, then burst into deep belly laughs. "I haven't heard that one for a long time." His mirth receded into chuckles, his wide smile crinkling up the lines around his eyes. "Have dinner with me tonight?"

"Can't."

"Why not?"

"I already have a date." Mentally, Robynn crossed her fingers to cross out the lie.

"You said before you'd spend the evening with me."

"Things have changed since then."

"I think I was trying to say I'm sorry for the way I acted this afternoon." He tried to capture one of her hands in his own.

"Dane, that has nothing to do with it." Robynn drew her hand back. *You could always go out to your folks' after dinner with him,* a sneaky little voice whispered in her ear. She shook her head. "I've got business to attend to."

"I thought you said you had a date." Like a big black cat hunting in a hay field, Dane pounced on her answer.

Her gaze flicked around the room, seeking escape. "I, u—m—um." She breathed in deep. Raised her chin. Looked him straight in the eye, her head at an imperious angle. The Princess completely hid the quivering woman.

"Can't you get the point? I don't want you taking care of me. I don't need you. And I'm busy tonight."

With a snort of disgust, Dane straightened off the wall. "I'll see you tomorrow then."

"Tomorrow's my day off."

"Good. I'll pick you up at two."

"I won't be home."

"Another date?"

"Yes, with the only really important man in my life."

"Robynn..."

Blue eyes clashed with violet. Sparks flew—enough to start a barn burning—but Robynn refused to back down.

Muttering something uncomplimentary under his breath, Dane strode across the carpeted floor.

"Talk about messing me up," Robynn mumbled to herself as she strolled back to Josh's room. "He causes more trouble than a boa constrictor at a ladies' luncheon."

A short time after saying goodnight to Josh, Robynn drove up on I-5, heading for Lake Oswego. Her parents had moved there several years ago, and while she always enjoyed the visits, the house had never seemed like home to her.

Robynn had also never asked them for money before. She had always stood on her own two feet, made her own way, even though at times she'd had to do without. Before in all the hard times but not so often the good times, whenever she *really* needed something, Robynn turned heavenward. *Like Mom says,* she reminded herself, *one good thing about calling God is that His line is never busy. Never get put on hold, either.*

Resolutely she shut the door on the voice that nagged her about only praying when she was desperate, but not before it reminded her that due to her lack of faith or expressions thereof, she didn't deserve an answer.

Her eyes watched the signs and traffic while her mind went into prayer mode—in spite of her. *God, Father, help. I need money. We want the horses so bad. Please give my dad a soft heart tonight so he'll want to buy in. Help me earn all the purses I need and find us some other backers.*

She shook her head. Why on earth was she praying? Pictures of Josh lying in the hospital brought on a guilty groan. For Josh she would do anything. *Father, I blew it again, didn't I? Josh's health is so much more important than money. Please heal him quickly. And I hate being at odds*

with anyone, especially Dane. Why did You bring him into my life? To help
now with Josh laid up? Is he the man You intend for me? If so, You'll have
to work it out. All I can see is problems. Thank You for never letting me go.

After the greetings at her parents' home, Robynn asked if she could
use the phone. "I need to call Jeremy. He was still at dinner when I left
home."

"Sure. Then let us talk to him." Her dad handed her the phone.

While waiting for Jeremy to come to the phone, Robynn filled her
mom and dad in on Josh's condition and what had been happening at the
track, carefully leaving out much about Dane. They already knew Josh's
nephew had taken over for him at the barns.

"Hi, Tiger, how ya doing?"

"Good; I can type on the Braille machine better all the time. My
teacher says I'm the best one in our class."

"Good for you. How's your reading doing?"

"Okay. Johnny is two books ahead of me in the contest. I got to catch
up."

Robynn laughed. "I'm sure you will. You're minding Mrs. C?"

"M–o–m!"

"Hey, just had to check. You want to talk with Grammy?" At his
enthusiastic response, she handed the phone to her mother. By the time
they'd all talked and she'd sent him a good-night kiss, the pang of being
parted had settled on her shoulders like half a mountain. His squeal when
she promised to be at the school to pick him up by ten in the morning
helped lift the load. Mondays with Jeremy were a high day of her week.

After her mother poured the coffee, Robynn laid out the plan she and
Josh had decided on. The next two hours went extremely well. Robynn's
parents, after an exchange of glances, decided that owning some up-and-
coming racehorses might be a lot of fun, besides being a good investment.
Robynn climbed back in her car with all their good wishes and the promise
of seventy-five thousand dollars in a week and another fifty thousand
dollars by the end of the year should they need it. Her father would also
check around for other backers.

"We've been praying for some way to help you out," her father said.
"Since you're so stubborn, maybe this is it."

Robynn watched her mother. She knew that the downcast eyes meant her mother was praying, most likely for wisdom. Robynn thought about telling them she'd prayed about this, too, knowing how they desired her to return to church and her Bible study. But it seemed manipulative, just like asking God for help had. If only—

She barely kept herself from shaking her head. If only's didn't count.

Robynn drove home in a daze. "Thanks, God," she finally whispered. "Seems like You really do care about what I care about, like Mom said. I've never seen You work so fast before." The dawning reality exploded in her mind. They would own the horses. A quarter of a million dollars didn't seem such an unreachable dream anymore.

Unable to wait, she swung her little car off at the exit to the hospital. Late-night arrivals were becoming a habit. She tiptoed down the darkened hall of the fifth floor and gently pushed open the door.

Josh turned his head at the slight sound.

"Not sleeping yet?" she whispered.

"No," came the gruff reply. "Got too much on my mind." "I know the feeling. I went to see my parents and . . ."

"Yes. Yes."

"And they'll enjoy being part owners of our horses. Dad's been looking for something new to get into and . . ."

"How much?" Josh squeezed her hand impatiently. "How much?"

"Seventy-five thousand dollars now and more at the end of the year."

"Well, and you wouldn't be ateasin' an old man, now would ye?" His hand gripped tighter.

"No, Josh." Robynn squeezed back, then removed her fingers to check for broken bones. "Things are looking better than a few hours ago."

"Saints be praised." He shook his head. "I never dreamed we'd get that kind of money from them."

"You get to sleep now." She smoothed the covers where she had been sitting. "I've got to get home. All of us can't sleep late in the morning like you."

"I can't believe it." He shook his head again. "Princess?" She turned back at the door. "Give Jeremy a hug for me."

Robynn blew him a kiss as she tiptoed out into the hall. She felt like an interloper in the darkened hospital. Signs on all the walls proclaimed the visiting hours were over at nine.

"Tough." She informed the down button on the elevator. "This news couldn't keep until morning."

The promised sunshine broke through the clouds the next morning to find Robynn easing back in her Celica, down the 1-5 freeway that was alive with braiding strands of traffic. Once past Wilsonville, the flat open country of the Willamette Valley, bound on both sides by mountains and hills, silently encouraged more speed. Robynn set the cruise control at fifty-nine. She didn't need another ticket. If she kept on like she had been going, she'd get known as a freeway jockey as well as a racetrack jockey. Major difference. Here *she* paid.

Robynn turned at the first Salem exit and followed the truck route until she saw the signs for the State School for the Blind. Whistling under her breath, she parked in the parking lot and reached in the backseat for the sack containing Jeremy's present. She knew she was trying to buy his approval when she brought a present each visiting day, but it didn't matter. He enjoyed the little surprises, and she enjoyed his enjoyment.

She glanced at her watch. Ten o'clock right on the button.

At the swinging glass door, she checked her appearance. Under her leather jacket she wore a red cashmere cowl-neck sweater because Jeremy loved the feel of it. Her gold chains were of different textures. He liked that, too. Even her perfume had been chosen with him in mind. It was Blue Grass, reminding her of open fields and warm sunny days. *People here will begin to think I don't own anything else,* she chuckled to herself as she swung the door open.

The tap of her high leather dress boots announced her arrival to the curly headed boy slumped in the leather chair even faster than her voice did.

"Mommy!" He was out of the chair like a shot and into her arms as she stooped to clutch him to her.

"Hey, Tiger." She hugged him again, aware that he wouldn't tolerate too much "mushy stuff." Today he didn't pull away. Instead he rubbed his cheek against the soft fleece of her sweater.

Robynn stroked his head, each ebony curl springing back into place after her fingers' passage. "How've you been?"

"Fine." He lifted his head. A smile curved his rosy lips and deepened the dimple in his cheek. "I've been learning on the Braille typewriter. Pretty soon I'll be able to write you a letter. I get to do it 'cause my teacher says I'm so smart." The last was said with a bit of a swagger.

"That's super-fantastic." Robynn sank down in the deep armchair in front of the windows. Today she wasn't aware of the book-lined walls. All her attention concentrated on the jeans-clad figure beside her. "What else you been doing?"

"Ah-h. I made my bed today without even being reminded. Mrs. C gave me a star." He squirmed on the seat beside her, already having sat his quota for the day. "Her dog had pups. She's gonna bring one after her day off."

"What kind?"

"Hm-m." He thought hard. "I think she called them labortory dogs."

Robynn grinned at him. "You mean Labrador?"

"That's what I said. Labortory. They're hunting dogs. Someday I'm gonna have a hunting dog." He turned so he faced her on the seat. One could never tell he was blind by looking into his sparkling blue eyes. "Did you know they give dogs to blind people to help them see? The dog takes them around. Mom, I'm gonna have one of those dogs someday. When I get lots bigger."

"Sounds like a winner to me. What gave you the idea?"

"They brought one to school. He wears a harness and everything. You shoulda been here."

Guilt made her flinch. "Maybe next time. You'll have to tell him to come on Mondays." Robynn picked up the package from where she had dropped it in the rush of greetings. "Brought you something."

Jeremy found the sack lying on her lap. He opened the top and reached inside to remove the soft, fuzzy bear.

"He's a koala bear," Robynn told him as his swift fingers explored the plush animal. "Koalas live in Australia, in eucalyptus trees. He has fur the color of dust and round black eyes."

Jeremy hugged the animal with one arm and took her hand with the other. "Where we going today? Mrs. C wants to talk with you. And my teacher says I can show you my lessons. That's this afternoon."

"Well, I thought maybe you'd like to go down to the park. The sun is shining, and it's beautiful out. Then we'll eat."

"At McDonald's?"

"At McDonald's. Aren't you getting tired of eating there?"

"Nope." He tugged on her hand. "Let's go. Now."

They spent the next couple of hours at the park on the swings and slides.

"Faster, Mom! Turn it faster." Jeremy shrieked on the merry-go-round. Robynn grabbed the bars as they came around and flung them away again with all her might.

"That's enough," she laughed. "I need to get my breath. I'll sit here, Son, and you ride it out."

Jeremy leaned back against the force of the spinning machine. His curls feathered in the breeze, and the red of his T-shirt reflected in his bright cheeks. Like Robynn, he lifted his face to the smiling sun, seeking its warmth. When the ride finally slowed to a stop, he slid to the edge, dragging his toe in the dirt and right through a shallow puddle.

"Hey! I'm wet!" He shrieked with joy.

"You would." Robynn laughed along with him. "How come I always take you back wet or muddy? You can find a puddle faster than a duck."

"Quack, quack." Jeremy strutted toward her, confident that she would watch out for him. All his life, he'd rather bump into things than have people baby him. The playground had become very familiar to him since they came here on the nice days.

"Ready to eat?"

"Can I have a Big Mac?"

"Is there anything else?"

"Yeah. You have Chicken McNuggets so I can have one of those, too."

By late afternoon, Robynn and Jeremy had finished all he had planned for them to do. While she watched him play with the other children, the woman in charge of the school came and sat down on the playground beside her.

"Jeremy is doing very well here," she said. "You can be proud of him."

"I always am," Robynn replied softly, never taking her eyes from the slim figure in red and blue.

"All the children like him because he has such a good sense of humor. I have yet to see him hit anyone else or get really angry."

"Beware when he does," Robynn said with a laugh. "He has a temper if you push him too far."

"He's proud of you, too. Says you're a jockey. Is that true?"

Robynn turned to smile at the motherly woman beside her. "Yes, it is. One thing you'll learn, Jeremy never lies. He might get his facts mixed up sometimes, but he never lies."

"His father is a jockey, too?"

"Was."

"Oh, I'm sorry."

"Don't be. Jeremy's father died before Jeremy was born. I've told him about his dad and so have others." Robynn clasped her hands about one raised knee. "It was a long time ago."

Dinner was served family style, and Jeremy led her to his table to sit beside him. Robynn was glad she had been so meticulous about teaching Jeremy to eat properly. Some of the children were still in the mess of learning.

By the time Robynn read him his *Cat in the Hat* book, Jeremy was cuddled in her lap, sweet smelling from his bath. His eyes drooped as she tucked him and his koala bear into bed. Robynn hugged him close. She kissed his cheek, then kissed him lovingly again. Wasn't he a bit warm?

"I'll watch him close!" Mrs. C, a white-haired lady with twinkling eyes assured her. "If there's any problem, we'll let you know right away. Maybe he just had an extra big day today."

Robynn chewed her lip as she swung out the front door. It would be so much easier on her mind if he were home where she could watch him.

"God, please watch out for him. I can't." Robynn unlocked her car and slid into the seat. "Please?" She rested her forehead on the steering wheel. Leaving Jeremy didn't get any easier. She thumped the wheel with the heel of her hand. They hadn't said his prayers, either. As she drove out of the parking lot, a thought repeated itself. *Why would you expect Jeremy to pray when you don't? He should be in Sunday school, too. Hmm.*

SEVEN

Robynn leaped out of bed, rejuvenated after her day off, even though she'd gone to sleep stewing about Jeremy and all the muddling aspects of her situation. *If you're not careful, my girl, she reminded herself, you're going to feel pulled into tiny pieces.*

Each time she began to worry, she thought again of the promised money from her father. It made the load seem easier.

And Dane. Keeping him out of her thoughts would be like trying to stop the bubbles from rising in a tub full of bubble bath.

The bubbles stayed with her all the way to the track. The stars were still bright with only the faintest line of dawn in the east when she locked her car in the parking lot.

"Where were you yesterday?" Dane barked as soon as he saw her.

Stunned, Robynn tried for a moment to remember. "I told you I would be gone all day." A tentative smile tugged at the corners of her mouth.

"Yes! You said 'with the only important man in my life.' But you didn't say you'd be gone all evening, too." He threw the gear he was carrying down on the tack boxes.

"I don't understand why you're so upset . . ."

"Upset! You call me upset! I must have dialed your number a thousand times. I finally went over there to make sure you were all right and the house was empty. Josh . . ."

"Josh knew where I was," Robynn interrupted his tirade.

That stopped Dane in his tracks. "He did?"

Maybe Josh is right flitted through her mind. He sure acts like a man worried half out of his mind. Maybe he really does care about me. Robynn O'Dell, the person, not just keeping a woman off his horses.

"Yes, he did." She gazed at him, the smile still hovering. "Did you have a good day?"

"Not particularly." A matching smile started in his eyes and tiptoed to his lips. "Did you?"

"Yes, a marvelous day."

"Are you going to tell me who with?" His jaw tightened again.

Robynn watched him for several moments. Doubt and indecision chased each other across her face before a smile banished them both. "Not just now." She paused. "But probably sometime. Sometime soon." *Why not now?* She consciously kept her thoughts from her eyes and face. The man was too perceptive by far. "I don't like to be hollered at."

"Then why. . .?" He paused and lowered his voice with visible effort. "Then why keep secrets from me?"

"Isn't that a bit like the pot calling the kettle black? Like you've not told me anything about yourself. And yet . . ." She sucked in a deep breath. "Forget it."

When he reached for her, she took a step back. "That isn't the answer, either."

"It is for me." He put both arms on the wall behind her, effectively trapping her between two walls, one of flesh and blood, the other solid wood.

Robynn let herself go limp. She would not respond to him, no matter what her jangling nerve ends screamed.

A horse whinnied. Another banged a forefoot against the door.

"I think I hear your friends calling us," she whispered.

"Is that what you call them?" Dane sighed and dropped his arms. "Then let's get going." His gaze bored into hers. "But we're not over this yet, not by a long shot."

Together they sauntered down the row of stalls bound by horses impatiently hanging their heads over the doors. Robynn greeted each one, giving special rubs and pats to her favorites.

As Dane gave her the instructions for each workout, he punctuated his words by tapping with one finger on her knee. The spot seemed eternally warm, even in the breeze from galloping through the early morning ground mist. The sun rising round and golden from behind Mount Hood inspired cheerful responses from all the people working at The Meadows. Grooms, trainers, bug boys, jockeys, everyone perked up, glad for a respite from the never-ending rain.

The good cheer extended into the afternoon's program.

The bantering between jockeys in the saddling paddock set laughter ringing against the high dusky ceiling. Robynn gave as good as she got. Dane was the recipient of secret, admiring glances from all the female contingent.

"Robynn, are you paying attention?" He spoke sharply to get her attention away from the sallies of the young jockey mounted next to her.

"Of course," Robynn sobered instantly. "I heard everything you said. Try to take him out in front from the beginning and . . ." She paused. "You realize I've ridden this horse many times. I think by now I know his little tricks better than anyone."

Dane glared up at her. "Just be careful."

"I will."

"I just bet." He led the animal out to the pony rider.

Being careful was not in Robynn's vocabulary today or any day. Her mount got off to a bad start. By the time he found his footing, the rest of the pack galloped a furlong ahead of them.

Robynn brought her stick down on his rump just once. The horse exploded and advanced on the pack like a steam engine out of control. A row of tightly packed haunches barred their way. Robynn tried to pull him up, but the horse laid back his ears and drove right down the middle.

"Coming through," Robynn yelled as she fought to get him back under control. Miraculously the horses parted without any clipping on either side. Robynn breathed a sigh of relief.

The field was clear until he caught the two front-runners neck and neck in the backstretch. Robynn guided him to the outside. He paced the leaders until she swung her bat again. With a surge, he drove for the finish line, winner by a nose.

Robynn caught the heat from Dane's snapping eyes as she slipped her saddle off the steaming animal. She smiled for the camera and nodded gracefully at all the accolades.

"That was some ride," the barrel-chested owner congratulated her. "You used real unusual strategy with him this time. Glad to see it worked." He pumped her hand again while the trainer took the animal back to the barn.

Robynn weighed in, and as she stepped from the scale, Dane let loose.

"I couldn't help it," Robynn responded when she finally got a word in edgewise. "Somehow he got the bit in his teeth . . ."

"Sheer carelessness on your part." The white lines around his mouth announced the effort he was making at control. "If you'd been stronger . . ."

"That has nothing to do with it. I've seen it happen to men, too. Just be grateful no one got hurt. I am." She turned on her heel and stomped off to the dressing room.

"Man, oh man," Pam commiserated once they were in the dull green room. "He sure let you have it. You going to put up with that kind of harassment?"

The sigh that escaped as Robynn sat down on the bench came clear from her toes. "He's just worried about my lily-white neck. I'm trying to ignore him."

"That ain't easy." Pam joined her, leaning against the concrete wall.

"You're telling me." Robynn leaned her head from side to side, trying to loosen the kinks. "That monster animal scared me out of ten black hairs. A few more like him, and I'll have lily-white hair to match my neck."

Pam chuckled. "Well, no one could tell by looking at you. Calm, cool, and collected as always."

"For that performance today I should get an Oscar."

"I wonder if they give Dane awards."

"Pam!"

Dane remained tight-lipped and surly the rest of the day. But he didn't try to tell Robynn how to ride each mount. In fact, he hardly spoke to her at all.

That evening when Robynn visited the hospital, Josh had good news for her. He had rounded up another twenty-five thousand dollars to invest in *our string* as he already called the horses.

"See," he chortled. "Even broken I'm good for something. Have some more guys coming to see me tomorrow."

"You kinda like having them come to you, don't you?" Robynn teased. "King Josh."

"How'd it go today? Sure wish they'd broadcast it on TV. Even the radio stations don't carry the races. I feel like I'm stuck here in no-man's-land and the track is only five miles away."

"Quit your grumping. I added another fifteen hundred dollars to the kitty today. The sun shining for a change brought out the best in everybody." She studied the cuticle of her thumb. "It's at times like this that I wish you could bet on my rides—see if we could up our investment money."

"You know better than that. You haven't forgotten our pact, have you?" Josh pointed at the chair. "Sit down so I don't have to strain my neck." She sat.

"No. I know that some Christians say betting is a sin, so we don't do it, but still. . ." She raised a hand as though stopping traffic. "Don't worry, Josh, I just said I thought about it. I'm not serious."

"Good." Josh relaxed back in his pillows. "Sounded to me like you and Dane had a bit of a set-to."

"Why? Oh. You talked to Dane already. He *was* a bit put out with me." She slid down in the seat.

"I'd call it more than a bit put out."

"I'd call it furious." Dane's deep voice announced his entrance.

Robynn sank lower in her chair. She winked at Josh and licked the smile off her lips. "Why, Dane." The honey dripped. "Fancy meeting you here."

"Now, you two are supposed to be getting along." Josh punctuated each word with a slash of his hand. "Am I gonna have to come over there and referee?"

Dane pulled a chair next to Robynn's and, when he sat down, leaned his arm along the back of her chair. Each time she moved her head, she could feel the brush of her hair against his sleeve. It made concentrating on the conversation increasingly difficult.

"Well, I've got to get going," she said as she broke into the first lull. "You behave yourself, Josh. Don't go sweet-talking the nurses." She glanced at Dane. "I'll see you in the morning."

"Have you eaten yet?" He stopped her with a hand on her wrist.

"No. I have stew in the slow cooker at home. Would you like to come for dinner?" The words slipped out before she had time to think.

"She makes a mighty mean stew, boy." Josh leaned back against his pillows. "You better take her up on it."

"I plan to." Dane slid his hand down to her fingers. "What are we waiting for?" He rose and almost pulled her from the room. "See you later."

He stuck his head back around the door and winked at the old man in the bed.

All the way home Robynn racked her brain, trying to think what else to have with the stew. Maybe a cottage cheese and pear salad, and there were home-baked rolls in the freezer. But what for dessert? She never had sweet stuff in the house. Too tempting. *Well, tough,* she finally decided. *He'll have to take what I have. Next time I'll plan a special meal.* She caught herself. Next time. Having Dane around was becoming a habit, a natural event. Was that the way love sneaked up on you? Day by day instead of fireworks and rocket explosions?

Dane's nearness caused her to fumble with her key at the door. The heat from his body permeated her jacket and clothing. Her nerve ends lit up like sparklers on the Fourth of July. Who said there were no fireworks?

The rich aroma of bubbling beef stew announced the menu even before they opened the door.

When Robynn turned to take Dane's coat after flipping on the lights, he pulled her into his arms.

"You know, I can't seem to keep my hands off you," he murmured into her fragrant hair.

"You'll have to if you want to eat." Robynn listened to his heart drumming under her ear. "Or aren't you hungry?"

"That's a tricky question." He smiled down into her upturned face. "Either way I answer it, I'll have to chew on my boot leather."

"Better chew on the stew instead." She pulled away from his embrace and opened the refrigerator door. "Here." She handed out containers. "I'll make the salad while you set the table."

At the perplexed expression furrowing his eyes, she laughed. "I'll tell you how."

"I know how to set tables." He grinned at her as she closed the door. "I thought you said I had to make the salad. I cook a mean steak and fry chicken better than the Colonel, but salads mean slicing veggies in tiny pieces. And slicing usually means blood—mine."

"Well, we certainly wouldn't want you bleeding all over the place, would we? The dishes are up there, and the silverware is in the drawer next to the dishwasher."

Robynn found herself touching Dane every time she passed him; little things like hands brushing, shoulders meeting, a hand on his arm. It was a good feeling, a right feeling. Working together like this in the evening after a day at the track made her day complete. Complete. That was the word. A part of her had been missing up until now; she just realized it. If only Jeremy could be here at home, too.

Life with Sonny had been razzle-dazzle, arguments and tears, wild reconciliations. The time with Dane, especially away from the track, grew like a river fed by small tributaries as it flowed deeper and broader.

"You're awfully quiet." He laid down his fork after finishing dinner. "Can you share the thoughts behind those beautiful violet eyes?" He waited for an answer.

"I–I. Dane, are you married?"

"Heavens, no. What made you ask that?"

"Well, Pam said I had to make sure." Confusion colored her neck to match her rose-colored shirt.

Dane's eyes narrowed, creases appeared on his forehead. "How do you figure I could be here with you like this if I were married? What kind of a man do you think I am?"

"Dane, I, um–m." Black lashes veiled her eyes, as a red stain rose to cover her cheeks. She felt hot all over. *What a stupid, stupid . . .* She swallowed. "Please," she whispered, one hand raised beseechingly. "I'm sorry."

"Robynn." Dane came around the table and took her hand. "We need to do some serious talking. I think the living room will be a better place."

When she looked up at him, she realized a smile had replaced the frown.

"Why don't you start the fire while I bring in the coffee? The matches are in the pottery bowl on the mantel." Dane nodded but seemed reluctant to release her fingers.

Robynn heard the sounds of fire building as she reached for the instant coffee. At the last moment she changed her mind and got out the jar of coffee beans instead. She dumped them in the grinder while filling the tank on her under-the-counter coffeemaker. Instantly, the aromatic scent of fresh coffee filled the air. Smiling to herself, Robynn piled the dishes in the sink, waiting for the pot to finish dripping. She entered the living room a few minutes later, carrying a pewter tray with hand-thrown pottery mugs on it.

Dane reclined in front of the now-roaring fire, orange and yellow flames casting dancing shadows over his pensive face. He had turned on the stereo so easy listening music played counterpoint to the snap and hiss of the burning logs.

"Sit here." Dane patted the spot in front of him. "I saved it just for you."

Robynn smiled as she handed him his mug. Then setting the tray on the coffee table, she surprised herself by doing just as he asked. Immediately he wrapped a strong arm about her waist and pulled her back to lean against the hard muscles of his chest. For a while they stared into the flickering firelight, sipping coffee, a feeling of peace and contentment floating on the strains of the music.

"Princess Lady."

"Um–m."

"What is there about you that's so different from anyone I've ever known before? You're feisty, fun, and funny; you make me furious, yet in the next moment I want to hold you."

He paused, allowing his thoughts free rein. "You're mysterious. One of these days I hope you'll let me in on those deep thoughts and hidden hurts." All the while he talked, his fingers drew hypnotic lines up and down her arm.

"But there's more than that. Things don't seem to get you down. There's a caring that flows out of you and touches everything around. Everyone at the track is so protective of you, I can't find out much of anything. Even Josh, my own uncle."

"What did he say?" Robynn scooted down so her head could rest on his arm.

"'Ask Robynn. When she's ready, she'll tell you.'" Dane set his cup down on the hearth. "I'm asking, love. I need to know."

"What's different about me?" Robynn stared into the fire, searching for the right words. "About that caring you said I have? It's not mine. My heavenly Father gives it to me, and I just pass it on. He's the one who keeps me steady, even when I forget to ask. My mom says He sends guardian angels, a whole platoon of them in my case, to watch over me. I like that idea. When things were really bad, when Sonny, the man I married at eighteen much against my parents' wishes, left me and then was killed the next day, I had nowhere else to turn. There's an old saying that has come to mean a great deal to me, 'When we share our sorrows they're cut in half. Share our joys and we double them.'"

"I like that." If Robynn had turned her head, she would have seen compassion and love on his face.

"To make a long story short, I am who I am because God lives up to His promises. When . . ." She paused, struggling with the idea of telling him about Jeremy. *Why don't I just tell him?*

"Robynn."

"Um—m—m."

"Look at me."

She turned her head. The moment for telling him passed. The look in his eyes made her heart speed up.

"I think I'm falling in love with you." The words hung in the air, crystal clear and perfect.

Robynn couldn't answer. She reached out with one hand, laying it gently along his jaw. Her fingertips rasped on the slight end-of-the-day stubble. With a small movement, he turned his face and, with his warm lips against warm flesh, bestowed a kiss in her palm. His eyes never left hers, holding her, cocooning her with their intensity. "That's why I can't stand to watch you race. Every time a horse falls, I see you under it. When a jockey is thrown, I'm sure it must be you."

"But . . . but I'm a good rider. Those things are just accidents. People get injured driving down the freeway just as easy—look at Josh. Besides, racing is my life."

"But accidents, as you say, can ruin a person's life." *Tell her about your mother,* his inner voice prompted. *If you want to know her secrets, you have to reveal yours.*

Tension crept into the room, snaking between them, flicking them with its ugly tongue. Dane's face assumed the tight-lipped expression he wore when pushed to the edge of his patience.

Tell her! The voice became imperative. *Tell her about Mother, about how you failed in the promise to your father.*

He rose to his feet. "Thanks for the dinner, Princess." He held out his hand to pull her up. "I'll see you at the track in the morning."

Robynn nodded, as a chill crept about her shoulder blades and settled around her heart, a chill that had nothing to do with the warmth of the room.

She handed him his jacket, then walked him to the door and stood shivering on the step until he started his car and backed out the drive. The shivers continued to attack her until long after she snuggled down under her warm comforter on the bed. "Why couldn't I say how I feel? Why couldn't I tell him about Jeremy? God, what's wrong with me?" She pounded her pillow, wishing it were her stubbornly disobedient mind.

The next morning, Dane's clipped voice gave her the training instructions, but there was no warm interlude in the tack room. It was as if he had put his emotions on hold. Robynn hoped it wouldn't be for long. She'd gotten used to the brush of his hand, the pressure under her elbow when he walked her to the cafeteria.

Robynn finished exercising the horses and left for the hospital to talk to Josh. Her afternoon program was full—eight rides.

"How's it going?" she asked as she entered the room. "You behaving yourself?"

"Can't do much else long as I'm hooked up to that contraption." Josh pointed to the weights and pulleys holding his heavy cast in the air. "Doctor says another week. Then they'll X-ray it again. And it better be a-healing, is all I can say."

"Well, as you always tell me, 'picture it the way you want it to be.' I'm sure that pertains to broken bones, too. And you know there are lots of people praying. First time for some of them."

"Thanks, lass. I know you have, and I do appreciate it." He pointed to a tablet on the table beside his bed. "There's the list of money we've been promised. Not as much as I'd hoped, but it could be worse."

"I'm on my way down to the loan officer at the bank to talk about a second mortgage on my house. If I can get fifty thousand dollars we should be in pretty good shape. I'm booked solid at the track. Winning makes everyone want me."

"You've been doing a fine job. How are you and Dane getting along? From the looks of the wins, you make a good team."

Robynn chewed her bottom lip as she studied the cuticles on her nails. Her hair waved forward, partially hiding her eyes.

"Dr. Rice to surgery. Dr. Rice to surgery" blaring from the intercom accented the silence in the flower-filled room.

"Oh, Josh." The words poured forth once she started. "He says he loves me but can't stand to watch me race. What am I going to do?"

"Do you love him?"

"I think so—oh, I don't know." She leaped from the chair and went to stand at the sink, her back to the man in the bed. "I couldn't say 'I love you' and I couldn't tell him about Jeremy." She turned, a desperate plea in her eyes, face, and voice. "What's the matter with me?"

"Give it time, lass." Josh used the same soothing tone with her as he did with high-strung horses. "Give it time. You're so impatient. If love is right, time never hurts it. Let it grow, lass, 'til the season is right." He paused. "Did he tell you anything about his family?"

She shook her head. "I've been meaning to ask, but something always comes up. I don't get it. Why? Is there something really important I oughta know?"

"You'll just have to ask him."

"You could tell me."

"I could, but I won't. Just like I haven't told him about Jeremy since you seem to want to keep that boy a secret." His eyes grew piercing. "Why?"

Robynn drew circles on the bedspread. "I–I think I'm afraid of Jeremy getting hurt. What if he really likes Dane and then this, whatever this is, is over? Men leave, you know. If I get hurt, stupid me, but I can't have Jeremy hurt."

"Thought it might be somethin' like that."

She sank down on the edge of the bed beside him. Tears shimmered in her eyes and deepened her voice. "Thanks, Josh. You're about the best friend anybody could ever have."

"Now get on with ye," his brogue thickened. "Or you'll have us both a-weepin'."

"Thanks again." She leaned over and kissed him lightly on the cheek, then was gone.

The loan officer was not as amicable as she had hoped. Even as he studied her credit references and her payment history at his own institution, the frown never left his forehead.

"You realize," he said, tapping the papers with a pen, "that you're in a very unstable profession. What if you were injured tomorrow and couldn't ride anymore? How would you pay this off?"

"If I were permanently disabled, my insurance would cover the mortgages on my home. Besides, we'd own some increasingly valuable horses." Robynn strove to appear businesslike and knowledgeable, but this was beginning to feel like begging. She hated begging.

He studied the papers some more. "With the market the way it is right now, I don't see that we can go with the full amount." He looked over his glasses at her. "The board approved a loan for twenty-five thousand dollars. Will that be satisfactory?"

No, it won't, Robynn wanted to shout. *I need the full amount.* She raised her chin in the unconscious gesture she used when dealing with officious people. "That will be fine. When can I sign the papers?"

"They'll be ready by Monday. Can you come in then?"

"Fine." *I'll just have to be late for Jeremy.* She could see no other way out. "I'll be here at ten."

As she rose, Robynn extended her hand. "Thank you for your time." The dishrag handshake did nothing to raise her impression of the man. "I surely hope you won't go broke over this." She turned and marched across the tiled floor, her boots tapping out her resentment.

By the time the afternoon's races were over, her mood hadn't improved much. She'd only been in the money three times, never in the winner's circle.

Back in the dressing room, she shrugged as she let the shower beat down on her back. Win some, lose some. Another day, another dollar. The platitudes didn't help.

You never seem down, whispered in her ear from the conversation the night before.

"That's all you know, Mr. Morgan." She shut off the shower. "I get down, but I never stay down. That's the difference."

By the time she dressed, brushed her hair out, and blew it dry, she found herself whistling under her breath. The tune had been playing on the stereo the night before.

Dane was in his usual place, holding up the wall, when she came out. A smile answered her jaunty grin, her shattered bits of peace drawing together like iron filings to a magnet.

"Dinner?"

"It'll have to be quick. I planned to go to church tonight." She didn't even try to repress the bubbles his nearness caused. They were together again, oh happy day.

He tucked her arm in his after taking her duffel bag and slinging it over his other shoulder. "Can I come along?"

"May I?"

"Let me change that. May I take you to dinner and then to church?"

"What about the horses?"

"All done, Your Highness. Anything else?" He pushed the door open and held it for her.

"Yes. Where are we eating?"

When they entered the sanctuary of the small brick chapel at seven, Robynn allowed the strains of the organ prelude to wash over her, restoring her tranquility in preparation for the service. Why had she let so much time pass since the last service she attended? As they sat down in one of the short wooden pews, she glanced at the man beside her.

He smiled, then pulled her arm through his, drawing her closer. The service opened with the congregation singing "Just as I Am," "Amazing Grace," and other old favorites. Robynn rejoiced to hear Dane's strong baritone, singing like the words were familiar.

When he saw the question on her face, he whispered in her ear, "Mother saw to it that we all went to church as children. I just haven't been for a while." At her nod, he finished his statement. "A long while."

When the white-robed pastor rose for the sermon, Robynn turned off the thoughts rampaging through her mind and tried to concentrate on what he said. Her conscious mind caught the last words, "And the greatest of these is love." Dane turned to watch her as the pastor spoke of married love, the love between a man and a woman. Blue eyes met violet. The look they exchanged spoke the words they couldn't say.

Robynn's heart sang along as the words of the doxology closed the service. As usual, God had met her and left her feeling blessed.

"Do you come all the time?" Dane asked as they walked back to his car.

"No." She shook her head, the fresh fragrance of her perfume wafting upward. "It's so easy to get out of the habit. I just know I have a need to be here all the time again. The sermon always seems written just for me—and I need that."

The ride back to her house deepened the feeling of contentment. At the door, when Dane raised his lips from hers, he stared into her eyes for a long moment. "I meant what I said last night. I love you, Robynn O'Dell, and I'll keep at it 'til one of these days I'll wear you down so you'll love me back." He laid two fingers against her lips before she could respond. "Goodnight, Princess." And he was gone.

Robynn let herself into the dark house, the rose-hued cloud she floated in making the lights unnecessary. In the living room she switched her recorder off. She would answer calls herself.

As she undressed for bed, she felt Dane's lips against hers again. "I love you." What beautiful words.

The phone rang. She glanced at the clock by her bed. Nine. She was going to bed early for a change. On the third ring, she picked it up.

"Mrs. O'Dell?" A gentle voice spoke. "This is Mrs. Cravens, Jeremy's housemother."

"Yes. Is something wrong with Jeremy?" Fear immediately tightened her throat.

"No, no, dear. Nothing serious. Jeremy has just been feeling under the weather and wanted to talk to his mother. Here he is."

Robynn waited until a small voice said, "Mommy?"

"Yes, Tiger. I'm here. What do you need?" Robynn made her voice soothing and warm.

"My head hurts and my tummy aches." The plaintive note in his voice tore at Robynn's heart. She steeled herself to be positive.

"It's not much fun to feel crummy is it, Son? I'm sure you'll feel better tomorrow. Did I tell you Josh is in the hospital? He broke his leg and has a huge cast."

Jeremy immediately perked up. "When's he coming to see me? Can I visit him in the hospital? Did you win today?"

Robynn chuckled into the receiver. "Didn't do quite so well today. And Josh can't come to see you for a long time, but maybe we can sneak you in to visit him. I'll check, and we'll plan on doing that on Monday. How's that sound?"

"Good. Mrs. C said I could have a popsicle. Any kind I want. I like banana best."

"Good night, Tiger. You go have your popsicle and sleep tight. I love you. Let me talk to Mrs. C again, please."

"Sure. Bye, Mom." Robynn could hear him saying in the background. "Mrs. O'Dell?"

"Please call me Robynn. Thank you for being so good to him. I wish I could be there. I can come if it would help."

"Now don't you worry. He'll be right as rain in a day or two. There's been several cases of some twenty-four-hour virus," the grandmotherly voice continued reassuringly.

"You'll let me know?"

"Of course, dear. Don't worry. Good night now."

"Bye." Robynn heard the dial tone before she hung up. What an empty sound.

EIGHT

Father, take care of Jeremy, please," Robynn entreated on her way to the track in the early morning hours. She gave herself a mental shake. After all, it was "only a virus."

As she locked her car, she forced her princess mask back in place. Head high, shoulders erect, she entered the gate with her customary smile for the guard.

By the third mount for the morning, she caught a puzzled look in Dane's eyes as he gave her instructions. She made sure her smile brightened and a tiny bit of sparkle found its way to her eyes. If she could just quit feeling guilty about being here when Jeremy needed her.

"Are you all right?" Dane hung onto the horse's reins.

"I'm fine, Dane." She smiled again. "Really." She could feel his gaze boring into her back as she trotted the horse out onto the track. Long years of habit helped her concentrate on the animals she rode when her desire was to be cuddling a sick little boy. That's what moms were supposed to do.

As soon as the horses were all snapped onto the hot walker, she dashed for the pay phone. When the school answered, she asked for Mrs. Cravens.

"He's much better this morning," the cheery voice reassured over the line. "He'll probably stay in bed today, at least for a while, but he ate a piece of toast for breakfast. The monkey is already asking for another popsicle."

Relief made Robynn lean against the wall. "Thank you, Mrs. C. You've just made my day. You don't think it necessary that I come down tonight then?"

"No, no, dear. Jeremy'll be fine. You have a nice day now."

After the conversation Robynn felt a nice day was a more likely possibility.

"Everything okay now?" Dane set his tray down at her table.

"Yes." Robynn bit into her toast. "Everything is just great." His warm glance sent the tingles racing to her fingertips.

By race time, Robynn realized the shutters had locked over Dane's features again. His stoic look could have been carved out of stone, the same granite that chipped off in his words. His glacier eyes refused to meet hers as he gave her the instructions for each race.

Robynn ignored what she disagreed with. She'd been riding these horses long before he arrived on the scene.

Ignoring his instructions got her in trouble that afternoon. Around the first turn, she found herself boxed in by straining Thoroughbreds and determined jockeys. The only way to keep from being knocked about was to pull her mount back. By the time he hit his stride again, the other horses ran far ahead.

"You should have gone for the outside like I said." Dane's words dripped ice water, when he stopped her on the way to change.

"I know. I know." Robynn stared down at the saddle in her arms. "I thought I could get away with it. He just wasn't quick enough out of the gate."

She could hear the bricks clinking into place on the wall building between them. When she raised her eyes to smile at him, he glared at her once more and marched back to the barns.

By the end of the afternoon Robynn had added more wins to her reputation, but none of the purses were large ones. The sweepstakes of the day found her with only a third place, nothing to brag to Josh about. Tame Adventure, the favorite for the big race, had pulled a muscle and had to be scratched.

When Dane appeared in the hall waiting for her, Robynn stopped, amazed. "What are you doing here?"

"I thought we could go visit Josh. And then we'll have dinner." He lifted the duffel from her shoulder.

"Which are you today, Jekyll or Hyde?"

"What do you mean?" The warmth from his fingers seeped through, just as if they'd never itched to shake her.

"Dane." She planted her feet, refusing to go any farther. "An hour ago you wouldn't even say my name without snapping, at me, and now we're friends again. This isn't making any sense to me; I don't like feeling caught at the end of a string like a yo-yo."

"I have an easy answer for that." He dropped the duffel at their feet and took both her hands in his. "Stop racing and marry me."

The silence stretched and stretched some more. Robynn stared deep into his eyes, searching out any chance at humor. Slowly she became aware of his thumbs, smoothing the backs of her hands. Marrying him would make her life so much easier. They could buy the horses and the farm. And he loved her. He kept telling her so, in fact, if persistence was any indicator … But did she love him? She loved the feeling of being held in his arms, she missed him if they were separated, she loved laughing with him, teasing him. But did she care enough to give up racing?

"I take it that's either/or." She finally whispered past the lump in her throat.

"I think so." He leaned back against the concrete wall, tucking her under his arm. "You could have gone down so easily out there today."

"I know that, and it was a stupid mistake. One I won't make again." She could feel the thudding of his heart through her fingertips as they played with the buttons on his shirt. Dane covered her hands with his, stilling the nervous actions, pressing them into his chest. Slowly, his eyes remaining on hers, he raised each slim hand to his mouth and breathed a feather kiss onto the palm. Then he closed her fingers over the caress and pressed them shut.

"Let's go see Josh."

Mist softened Robynn's gaze at the tenderness Dane shared with her. Now would have been as good a time as any to mention Jeremy, but the words just wouldn't come. *Either/or, what would she do? Was there really any question?*

When Dane left Josh's room for a moment, she called Jeremy's school. Mrs. C reported that Jeremy had been good all day but had been so tired he fell asleep at dinner.

"Having a bug like this takes a lot out of the little tykes," Mrs. C stated positively. "I wouldn't worry none."

It's easy to say "don't worry," Robynn thought when she recalled the report on Jeremy as she undressed for bed that night. *You're there where you can watch him, and I'm up here, wishing I were beside him. It's a good thing he's been so healthy. The only illness he's had was the chicken pox a couple of weeks ago. I couldn't handle this on a regular basis.*

Robynn had come home for her break and was nearly ready to dash out the door at noon the next day when the phone rang.

"This is Mrs. Taylor. I spoke to you the other day when you visited Jeremy here at the school. I don't want to alarm you, but I have some bad news. I just took Jeremy into emergency at Capital Hospital. He started vomiting about eight last night."

"Oh, no." Robynn slumped against the wall.

"The doctor said to bring him in. I think you should come as soon as possible."

"Yes, I will." Robynn checked her watch. "I'll be there in about an hour." The phone clattered in the cradle. Wildly Robynn stared around the room, trying to decide whom to call.

Fingers shaking, she dialed Josh's number. "Josh, there's been an emergency. The school just called and Jeremy's in the hospital. They don't know what it is, but I'm leaving right away. Can you call my parents for me? I'll be at Capital Hospital."

"Of course, lass. Sure and you'll be wanting to let Dane know."

"You tell him; I can't right now. And Josh, pray hard."

"That I will. Robynn?"

"Yes." She shifted impatiently, wanting, needing to be on the road.

"You drive carefully."

"Thanks. I'll call you when I know something."

The drive down the freeway passed in a blur of fence posts, fields, and semi-trucks. Her shiny black car wove in and out of traffic expertly, even though its driver could hardly see through her tears.

"Father God," she muttered over and over. "Please take care of him. Make him well again. Why, oh why wasn't I there?"

What more could you have done? The calm, sensible side of her brain argued with the nagging guilt attacking her on the other.

Robynn stopped at the first gas station after turning off the freeway to ask directions to the hospital. Grateful for the lack of patrols on the streets, she sped through town, swung into the parking lot of the ancient brick hospital, and followed the signs to emergency.

The few seconds from the time she parked the car until she entered the automatic door played in slow motion.

"I'm Robynn O'Dell. They brought my son Jeremy in from the school for the blind?"

The nurse smiled up at her. "Yes, we've admitted him. You go over to the elevator," she pointed down the hall, "and up to three. Turn right."

"Thanks," Robynn called over her shoulder as she trotted along the narrow hall.

She repeated the procedure at the nurse's desk on three. The young, blond nurse in a red-checked smock didn't need to check her chart. "He's in 304," she said. "We're just getting him into his bed. Go right on in."

Strange, Robynn thought as she pushed open the door. *Two of the people I love most are in hospitals at the same time.*

Jeremy's face, except for the purple shadows under his eyes, almost matched the sheets. An IV had already been started in his arm, and the nurse was just finishing taking his blood pressure and temperature.

"How is he?" Robynn sank onto the edge of the bed beside him and smoothed the tousled hair back from his forehead. "Jeremy, Mommy's here." His blue-veined eyelids flickered.

"He's a pretty sick little boy." The nurse lifted a thin arm to check the pulse. "Little kids like this dehydrate pretty quickly, but the IV helps right away."

"Do you know what's wrong?" Robynn wanted to pick him up and hold him. He looked so small and fragile lying there.

"We're not sure. The blood work is down at the lab now. Your doctor should be in shortly. His name is Dr. Prescott, the pediatrician who takes care of the schoolchildren." She slipped her stethoscope back in the pocket of her cheery yellow top. "Can I get you anything?" she asked as she walked out. "A cup of coffee or a pop?"

"No. No, thank you." Robynn never took her eyes from the sleeping form.

When Jeremy's face contorted with the dry heaves, Robynn grabbed the basin from beside his pillow and held it for him.

"Oh, Jeremy," she muttered. "Jeremy, please get well." She wiped his mouth with a washcloth dampened at the sink. "Mommy?" A tiny whisper rewarded her efforts.

"Yes, darling, I'm here." She gathered him in her arms and hugged him close. "We're at the hospital so you can get better."

"Mrs. O'Dell?" A robust, gray-haired man with a crew cut stopped at the foot of the bed. "I'm Dr. Prescott." His warm smile inspired confidence immediately. "The blood work isn't back yet, but we started the IV to get some fluids back in him. The school gave us all the information we need. They mentioned that he had chicken pox about two weeks ago?"

"Yes." Robynn nodded. "A very light case. He had only about a dozen pox. He was only sick about a day. Do you think there's some connection?"

"We'll know more later. You didn't give him aspirin by any chance, did you?"

"No. He was at school. I came down the first two days. Then he was all right, just itched." She watched as the doctor checked Jeremy's pulse with thumb and forefinger, then eye responses with a tiny flashlight. "They said last night he just had a virus."

"And that's most likely what it is." Dr. Prescott nodded. "There's been a lot of stuff going around." He walked to the door. "Get him to take fluids if you can. Fruit juice, popsicles, anything. Just ask the nurses for whatever you need."

"Thank you, Doctor."

"I'll let you know as soon as we have some results." Robynn nodded as he left the room.

"Hey, Tiger." She patted the pale little face. "How about a piece of ice? You've always liked to munch ice chips." When he nodded the tiniest bit, she poured a couple pieces of ice into the paper cup and held it to his mouth.

"It's cold," he whispered around the crunches.

"I should hope so." His weak response made her feel giddy. "It'd be a real shame if ice were hot. How about some more?" A few more chips disappeared before the boy shook his head. Robynn felt like she'd earned her mother badge for the day. At least her being here had a good effect on him.

"Where is she?" Dane stopped at the foot of the bed. The tone of his voice matched the thunder on his brow.

"She had an emergency, like I told you." Josh smacked a pillow behind his head so he could see better. "Come over here so I don't get a crick in my neck from trying to see you."

Dane complied. "I swear I'll crank up that apparatus if you don't tell me." He pointed to the weights and pulleys holding Josh's leg up.

"Now, don't go gettin' all testy."

"You want *testy,* you just . . ."

"Sit down and behave yourself. Yer worse'n a horse with colic."

Dane took the chair he'd been pointed to and clasped his hands, elbows on his knees. He leaned closer to Josh. "Now, tell me."

"Jeremy is in the hospital in Salem, and she went to him."

"Jeremy?"

"Her seven-year-old son."

Dane leaned back like he'd been pushed. "A son? Why hasn't she told me? Why . . . ?"

Josh sighed. "Why haven't you told her about your mother?"

"Touché." It was Dane's turn to sigh. "Is he—Jeremy—going to be all right?"

"I sure pray to God so. Something happens to that boy, and I don't know how she could stand it. They're at Capital Hospital in Salem. You might spend your driving time praying for them."

"I will. Thanks, Uncle." Dane stopped on his way out the door. "Don't tell her I'm coming, okay?"

"Just get going, and give her a walloping big hug from me."

Dane found her about an hour later, stretched out on the bed, cuddling the little boy to her, both of them sound asleep. Without a sound, he sat down in the chair and waited.

Robynn awoke when the nurse came in to change the IV bag. The nurse checked Jeremy's pulse again while Robynn scrambled from the bed, an apologetic look on her face. "I just wanted to hold him, but the tubing wasn't long enough. This seemed the next best thing."

"Don't worry, Mrs. O'Dell. We don't stand on rules so much in this department; whatever helps these little ones get well."

Robynn turned to find the chair only to encounter a familiar male form rising to meet her.

"Dane," she breathed. "When did you get here?"

"Quite some time ago, but I couldn't bear to wake you. The picture the two of you made—he's beautiful, Robynn, just like you." He paused, lifting a tentative hand to brush back the ebony wings of hair framing her face. "Why didn't you tell me about him?"

Anxiety wrinkled the creases around her eyes.

"I—I." Robynn fought the conflicting emotions warring to come out. "I . . ."

"Mommy?" At the thready whisper, she spun back to the bed.

"I'm here, darling, what is it? How about more ice? A popsicle?" The little hand clung to hers.

Jeremy nodded. "Banana."

"I'll see if they have it." Dane touched her shoulder reassuringly as he left the room.

"Do you want a piece of ice in the meantime?" Robynn noticed the little animal sitting on the window ledge. "I see they brought your koala bear." A tiny smile lifted the corners of Jeremy's mouth.

"Bear's my friend."

Rejoicing at any response, Robynn stood. "I'll get him for you." As she glanced out the window, her attention was caught by a stone statue of the shepherd and his sheep, banked about with scarlet chrysanthemums. "Thank You, Jesus," she whispered. "You're always here, every time I need You. And this is certainly a time of need."

She had just finished tucking the fuzzy koala under the covers, with Jeremy's arm locked around it, when Dane entered the room, triumphantly waving a yellow popsicle.

Robynn cracked it in half on the lip of the bedside table and, unwrapping it, held half to Jeremy's mouth. A tiny nibble followed another until much of it was gone. The grins that Dane and Robynn shared united them with one more silk-fine thread in the web of companionship.

The nurse brought in a dinner tray for Jeremy, but it remained untouched.

Awhile later a rounded woman with little pepper left in her hair hugged her daughter as soon as she entered the room. "Oh, Robynn, darling. We came as soon as we could." As Mary Ahern turned to her grandson, Robynn leaned against her father's chest.

"There now, girl." He patted her back. "It'll be all right. You'll see." Giving her another reassuring hug, he went around the bed to stand at Jeremy's other side.

"Grammy and Grandpa are here, Tiger. Can you wake up for them?"

Jeremy moved his head restlessly on the pillow, a frown caterpillaring his eyebrows.

Robynn stood back so that the grandparents could murmur words of love to their only grandson. Without a thought, she slipped her arm into Dane's. She leaned her head against his upper arm, the muscles contracting as he pressed her hand against his side.

"Mother, Father," Robynn said when they straightened, "I'd like you to meet Dane Morgan." Her voice had a proud ring to it. "He's my . . . uh . . . taking over for Josh. He's the nephew."

The three exchanged names and handshakes as Robynn thought, *friend? That's not enough. Boyfriend? He would like to be, but not yet, if ever. Here I am stuttering and stammering like some fifteen-year-old with her first date.*

"Have you had anything to eat?" Dane whispered in her ear as the grandparents turned their attention back to the silent form in the bed.

"No." Robynn shook her head.

"Did you eat at all today? You weren't at the cafeteria this morning." Robynn wrinkled her forehead trying to think.

"I'm not sure. All I could think of was Jeremy . . ."

"Why don't you come down to the cafeteria with me while your parents are here to watch him? You've got to take care of yourself, too."

"I can't leave until the doctor's been here."

Dane nodded and went out to the hall, returning a few minutes later with two more chairs. "Might as well wait comfortably."

When the doctor did arrive, he hadn't much more to say. Maybe by tomorrow the tests would be more conclusive. But perhaps then Jeremy would be much better.

Leaving her mother strict instructions to get liquids into her grandson, Robynn allowed Dane to lead her out the door.

After everyone left that night, when Robynn snuggled down in the chair-bed that Dane found, she reviewed all the things he did to make this disaster easier for her. Whatever she needed, he seemed to provide before she could ask. As if she would ask. She'd have done it herself. This depending on him was getting to be a habit. She watched Jeremy breathe, the dim light from the hall their only illumination. A very nice habit.

She awoke each time during the night when a nurse came in, but only once was she able to get Jeremy to take anything. Morning found her tired and rumpled.

The look of concern on Dr. Prescott's face did nothing to make her feel better. "The tests this morning showed a rise in blood ammonia and a drop in blood sugar. That confirms my earlier fears. Jeremy has Reye's syndrome, a rare complication to some common viruses like chicken pox and flu. Some schools of thought are that aspirin may contribute to this. That's why I asked you earlier if you had given Jeremy any. But neither you nor the school gave aspirin, and the theory's controversial. That's why I tell my patients to use Tylenol just to be safe. Whatever the cause may have been, Jeremy's diagnosis is definite."

"What does that mean?" Robynn took a deep breath. "What happens next?"

"If he doesn't go comatose on us, he'll have a better chance of recovery."

"Are you saying . . ." Fear wrapped its ugly claws around her stomach and jerked. "Are you saying that Jeremy might . . . might . . . die?" The impossible word was out.

"Not if I can help it. The problem is that we can only do what we're doing. We'll start a glucose solution stat to keep his blood sugar elevated, and then we wait. Are you a praying person?"

Mutely, Robynn nodded.

"Then I suggest you bombard the lines to heaven. We never know why one makes it and another doesn't." He picked up Jeremy's hand to take the pulse as if to give himself something to do. His dark eyes warmed with compassion.

"But it doesn't make any sense." Robynn sank into the chair, the load beating her down.

"No, it doesn't. But remember, he has as good a chance as any. He's basically a healthy little boy. His school says he's done well dealing with his disability. Maybe that has given him extra staying power. He'll need it." He paused as he turned to go. "Has the chaplain been in yet?"

When Robynn shook her head, he said, "I'll send for him."

Too numb to even say "thank you," Robynn stared at the slight figure in the bed. *God, it isn't fair,* her mind raged. *You can't have Jeremy. I need him worse than You do.* Tears rolled down her cheeks unheeded.

She got herself together enough to call her parents and Josh, sharing with them the most positive side of the prognosis, holding inside the fear, the anger.

"The doctor says to pray; call anyone else you can think of. I'll let you know if there's any change."

She hung up and went to stand at the window, staring at the statue. It reminded her of a verse from childhood: "I am the good shepherd. I know my own and my own know me." Comforted, Robynn turned to fight the battle.

By evening when Dane appeared at the door with a suitcase for her, Robynn had gotten some ice and another half a popsicle into Jeremy. Each bite he took was a victory in her mind.

"Josh told me," Dane said as he took her in his arms. Robynn clung to him, grateful for his caring.

"Thanks for bringing my things," she murmured into the comforting wall of his chest.

"Who's riding for me?" she asked after he had forced her to eat the food he brought on a tray. Some color had returned to her cheeks.

"Pam. And everyone sends their love. Why, there are people praying up there who only used God's name as an expletive before. They really care about the two of you."

Tears sprang to the corners of her eyes. She tightened her lips, willing herself not to cry. "Thank them for me, please." She stared down into her coffee cup. "And thank you for all you've done."

"Ah—h, Robynn," he pulled her onto his lap. "I've done so little when I want to do so much." Robynn curled there, comforted by the steady thud of his heart until Jeremy stirred restlessly. It was back to the fray again.

During the long night, Robynn alternated between sleeping in the chair-bed, caring for Jeremy, or pleading for his healing in the chapel.

"It's not fair, You know," she said at one point, feeling more like screaming. "You have lots of kids, and I only have one. You know You can heal him." The tears threatened to overwhelm her again. "And I–I know it, too." Her voice sank to a whisper. "But will You?"

She knotted her fingers together, as if the very action would keep her from flying into fragments. "God, he's *my* son. Please, please, don't take him from me." She stood and paced again, furious, wanting to shake her fist in His face. Her heels clicked against the tiled floor. She couldn't go back to Jeremy while she still felt like screaming. The rage erupted in chest-tearing tears, and she sank to the floor, her arms on the railing in front of the small altar. The cross hanging on the wall above drew her gaze when she could finally see again.

A voice, soft as a sigh, seemed to circle around her. *I lost My Son, too, for a time. I let Him die for you so that now you are My own. I will not let you go, nor ever forsake you. Come, rest in Me.*

"God, what else can I do?"

The picture of the shepherd statue came to her mind. *I am the good shepherd. I know my sheep and my sheep know me. Come my child, and rest in me.*

"But Jeremy . . ."

Just rest.

The next day Jeremy never even flinched at the ringing of the phone anymore. Dane called, then Josh not much later, and in the afternoon, her mother and father called to say they'd be down to be with her before long. She hung up to go stand at the window and look down at the shepherd. *Oh, God, you say Jesus is the shepherd of the sheep, but He doesn't seem to be here right now, when we need Him.*

Yes, I am here; I said I would never leave you nor forsake you. Just close your eyes and be with Me.

Robynn sank down in the chair, closing her eyes in both weariness and despair. The monitors bleeped along, shoes squeaked in the hall, and a voice called for someone over the loudspeaker. But Robynn felt like she was cradled in the softest down, and the heart she heard beating was not her own. She'd never felt so warm and comfortable—and comforted.

"God, please hold Jeremy like this." She wasn't sure if she whispered the words or only thought them, but she meant them with all of her heart.

"You look better, dear," her mother said when they arrived.

"I know." How could she tell them what she'd sensed? And yet she knew she wasn't going out of her mind. She'd never forget that sensation of perfect peace.

"How's our boy?" Her father touched his knuckles to Jeremy's cheek. "Come on, Tiger, we got things to do, places to see."

Robynn fought the tears that threatened to run at the sight of her father weeping without a sound. Her mother sat down on the bed and took Jeremy's left hand in her own.

"Just Grammy saying I love you and I baked your favorite cookies this morning. Brought some in case you were feeling better, but there's lots in the freezer waiting for you." She smoothed the lank hair back from Jeremy's forehead. "How about a popsicle? I checked, there's banana."

Jeremy blinked his eyes and gave the tiniest nod.

Robynn let her mother and father do the honors, knowing how much it meant to them to be able to do something. That was the hardest part, not being able to *do* anything.

"Let's go to the chapel," Dane suggested later, after he'd been there awhile. At Robynn's nod, he took her arm, and nodding to her parents, they walked down the hall.

The room waited, serene and calm as the picture on the wall. Candles flickered in squat, square glass holders that someone had left on the carpeted riser. Robynn walked into the second oaken pew from the front and took a seat sideways so she could see Dane. He sat down beside her and rested his wrists on the pew back in front of them and stared at the picture. The silence didn't beg for words but instead bestowed peace.

"He's about the same, then?"

His voice caught her by surprise. "Yes, I'd say so." Could she tell him about what had happened to her earlier?

"And you?" He reached with one finger and brushed back a lock of hair from her cheek. "You look better." The way he stared into her eyes seemed to plumb the depths of her being.

"I am. Dane, I think God held me in His arms this afternoon."

"Um—m." He nodded. "I've heard of things like that. My mother . . ." He stopped.

She waited.

"I'm glad for you."

He took her hand and rubbed the palm with his thumb. "Do you feel like talking?"

What does he want to talk about right now? Her throat clenched. Robynn blinked. "I—I guess. Is . . . is Josh all right?"

Dane snorted a little. "Can't keep him down. Pretty soon they'll pay me to take him home." He turned with one bent knee on the seat between them. "I. . ." He sighed. "I looked up Sonny O'Dell in the *Oregonian* and read about the accident and all. I hope you don't mind."

Robynn shook her head. "No, that's all history." She almost flinched at the grip he had on her hands.

He saw that and relaxed his fingers. "Could you . . . would you please tell me about you and Jeremy after that?"

And so she did, starting with when she knew she was pregnant, buying a house with the insurance money, and her shock at learning that her perfect baby boy was blind. "The doctors did all kinds of tests, hoping they could change the diagnosis with surgery." She shrugged. "But they couldn't. Mom and Dad helped care for him while I raced, and then when he got old enough, the doctor suggested I send him to a school for the blind to learn Braille and other skills he needs."

She paused, keeping her gaze on their joined hands. "I wonder if that was the right thing to do, especially now." Her eyes swam with tears as she looked up at him. "But it seemed right at the time."

"Hindsight is always twenty-twenty. That's what my mother says."

"I know." She waited again.

"I'd like you to meet my mother. She'll love Jeremy—and you."

Robynn canceled the thought that tried to take hold. *If Jeremy lives.*

"Where does she—your mother—live?"

"In Pasadena, not far from my house." Now it was his turn to pause. When he looked up, he took a deep breath and let it out. "My mother lives in a wheelchair, and it is all my fault." The words came out in a rush, as though if he didn't say them fast, he wouldn't say them at all.

"Your fault? Was there a car accident or . . ."

He shook his head. "My father died in Vietnam, but before he left, he told me to take care of my mother. She and her mount went down in a steeplechase and she never walked again."

Robynn waited for him to go on. When he didn't, she squeezed his hands. "How old were you when your father left?"

"Seven."

"And at the accident?"

"Ten." He looked up at her, eyes dark with suffering. "I saw her fall. That's why I don't want you racing. What if the same thing happens to you?"

Robynn blew out a breath of air and shook her head. "Dane, you were a kid, she was an adult. She *chose* to steeplechase."

"Like you choose to flat race." He leaned forward. "Jockeys are injured and killed all the time. I can't bear the thought of seeing you under some horse's hooves."

"Robynn, Jeremy's asking for you." Her mother stood in the doorway.

Robynn got to her feet. "We'll continue this discussion later, my friend." She cupped his cheek in her hand for a brief moment and then led the way back to Jeremy's room.

"Bear?" Jeremy opened his eyes half-mast. "Thirsty."

Robynn snuggled the bear in the crook of his arm and slid some ice chips between his parched lips. While he munched, she smoothed some lip balm around his mouth. When Dane returned with a popsicle, they got him to take part of a half.

After they all left, Robynn stood again at the window. This time her prayers were for another boy, one who had grown to become a wounded man. "Ah, Father, the loads we all carry. Why can't we let You carry them, like You want?"

By the fifth day, Jeremy's delirium alternated with restless sleep. The purple strokes under Robynn's eyes and the lines about her mouth shouted her condition, even if one ignored her trembling hands. But now she knew where to find sanctuary, clinging to the promised rest.

Dane found her in the chapel, kneeling in front of the picture of Christ with hands raised in welcome. Her mother and father were with Jeremy.

"Dane," she whispered in a broken voice as he gathered her in his arms. "I can't even think anymore. I just keep putting one foot in front of the other. I don't even know what to pray."

"Then that's the time the rest of us pray for you." He kissed away the moisture on her eyelids. *Can I pray aloud for her—right now?* Dane cleared his throat and sniffed. "Father in heaven, thank You for the strength You have given Robynn. Thank You for the healing You are bringing to Jeremy. Thank You that You have brought this woman into my life and through her, You've brought me back to You. Forgive me for taking off on my own instead of letting You be Lord of my life. Please give us wisdom and comfort and the peace that I have sensed in here."

Robynn sniffed and added her "amen."

"I wish I could stay here with you." He held both of her hands, his thumbs rubbing the fragile skin on the backs. "But with Josh in the hospital . . ."

"There's not a whole lot you can do here, and keeping real busy makes the time go by faster." She stood on tiptoe and kissed his cheek. "Thanks for the hugs and the prayer." She watched him head down the hall to the elevator.

During the next day, Jeremy tossed restlessly and refused everything she offered. Even being held in her arms didn't pacify him. By evening the lethargy had returned, deeper than before. The doctor and nurses had a harder time being optimistic.

"How much longer can he go like this?" Robynn asked as Dr. Prescott finished his examination.

"I don't know." He pressed her hand as he left the room.

"There comes a time," the slender, soft-voiced chaplain said when he met her in the chapel that night, "when we must place our children in God's hands, resting in the assurance that He knows best."

"I thought I did that when Jeremy was baptized and then again when we discovered he was blind. I'm learning to trust Him all over again, but . . ."

"That's part of the problem," he replied. "That 'but' is always there. Remember He promised to be with us, to deliver us from evil, to bear our burdens. There are no accidents with God, and He cares about our every incident, every tiny thing. Nothing is too small for Him or too hard. And He uses it all."

"So, if I had been more faithful, you think this wouldn't have happened to Jeremy?" Admitting this fear took all the power she had.

"Oh, no, I'm not saying that. Our merciful God doesn't work that way—but He is using this illness to draw you closer, is He not?"

Robynn nodded. "For so long I've felt alone, but not now."

Robynn couldn't sleep that night. She heard nothing but each slow breath Jeremy took, each one seeming farther apart. At three she found herself at the window, looking down on the lighted statue. "But God," she whispered against the windowpane, "I raised him for living, not for dying." A peace wrapped around her, seeping inside to quiet her soul.

The morning nurse confirmed Robynn's tentative hope. Jeremy seemed more alert. His blood test came back positive. The poison was leaving his system.

"Oh, Dane." The joy in her voice bubbled over the wire when Dane called. "Thank God, he's better. Tell everyone Jeremy's better. Now they can thank God along with us. Our boy is going to get well."

"That's wonderful. I love you, Princess." She could hardly understand him for the tears clogging his throat.

Jeremy was home by the end of the week to finish recovering before he returned to school. He was so weak he could hardly lift his head after the drive. The smile on his face tore at the hearts of the adults rejoicing around him.

"You're going to bed, my girl, for twenty-four hours straight," Dane ordered as he picked up his coat that evening. "Your mother is dying to take care of Jeremy and you, too. Let her do it."

When she didn't respond, he tilted her chin up with one finger so he could look into her eyes. "Hear me?"

"Who appointed you my keeper?" The sparkle had returned to her eyes.

"Me."

Her lips parted as his mouth descended to hers. When his arms came around her, she leaned into the strength of him, savoring the fresh scent of his aftershave. Talk about bulwarks in a storm, he had been one. The words of his prayer had never left her mind. Was God using this to get to other people, too—not just her?

NINE

Robynn's crystal bottle of joy shattered about her feet the next morning when she went to see Josh. One look at his face and she knew the news wasn't good.

"The farm is sold," Josh responded in answer to her query, "along with the brood mares and foals. Opal gave us an extension on the racing string but received too good an offer on the others to pass it up."

"But . . . but . . ." Robynn slumped down in the chair. "I was hoping for the breeding stock along with the racing string. I knew the farm was an impossible dream. But the colts . . ."

"It's sorry I am to be telling you such bad news. At a time like now, you should be rejoicing. Just think, lass, Jeremy's getting well again."

"I know." The sparkle returned. "I'll just be grateful for what is and not worry about tomorrow."

She rose and went to stand at the window. Seen from the south side and in the daylight, the arching white Fremont Bridge was still an awesome monument to man's ingenuity. The huge grain elevators down on the river were obscured by the criss-crossing freeways. "You had X-rays last week, didn't you?"

"Yes. And the bones are knitting together, but slowly. Said it was because of my age." Josh snorted at the thought. "He just wants to keep me in this contraption for as long as possible."

"Well, you've gotta admit it's kept you out of trouble. You know if you could hobble on crutches, you'd be down at the barns, telling everyone what to do."

Josh tried to glare at her, but his white hair every which way made him look more endearing than angry.

"I'm sorry I wasn't more help with the boy," he said. "Can you bring him to visit me soon?"

"Will they let him in?" She pulled one of the roses out of a fresh arrangement and held it to her nose.

"Don't ask, just do it as soon as he's feeling up to it. Why don't you take some of these flowers home with you? Let 'em smell up *your* house."

"You old faker." Robynn laughed. "You know you love all the attention. And roses have always been your favorite flower."

"Yours, too."

"Aye. But mostly around the neck of a horse." She scooped up a vase of red roses and, waving, left the room.

Well, she reminded herself philosophically when visions of the farm clouded her memory. *You can't win 'em all, and this way we have time to come up with less money. I've got to get back to work. Better notify my agent to get me back on the ponies day after tomorrow. That gives me one more day with Jeremy.*

"Who is that man that comes?" Jeremy asked the next morning. Dane had come for coffee the night before, after Jeremy's bedtime.

"His name is Dane Morgan, and Josh is his uncle. He's been taking Josh's place at the track, training the horses. Remember, I told you at the hospital. Why?" Robynn mashed his soft-boiled egg with a fork and seasoned it. "There, sir, your breakfast is ready." She walked to her own chair and sat down. Carefully, Jeremy held the bowl in place with one hand and spooned up the egg with the other. Robynn naturally placed all his food in the right order so he could easily locate each item.

Jeremy put his glass of milk back on the table, a white mustache decorating his upper lip. "'Cause I think he likes you."

"What gives you that idea?" Robynn kept her voice noncommittal, but her heart cartwheeled in her chest.

"He calls me Tiger and you Princess Lady. Is he going to be my new daddy?"

"Jeremy!"

"Well, other kids get new daddies, and my old one died so . . ." It was the classic case of the seven-year-old explaining the facts of life. Robynn felt properly put in her place.

"Finish your breakfast. Grammy will be here soon."

"I don't want any more." He got down from his chair. "Do we have any popsicles?"

"Beat it, monkey." Robynn smiled at the privilege of having her pint-sized philosopher home again. He might not be able to see with his eyes, but he sure viewed the world in his own special way.

The next two days set the pattern for Robynn's days. She arrived at the track by five; exercised as many horses as she could fit in, not just the string Dane ran; home by eleven for lunch and time with Jeremy; and back to the track to ride as many mounts as she could find in the afternoon program. Her evenings she devoted to Jeremy. Each night she read him a Bible story before his prayers, just like they used to. The only way Dane got to talk with her was to come over to her house. Their miniature chaperon was always present, ready to be part of the party.

Purple smudges appeared under Robynn's eyes again. But no matter how tired she was, she continued reading the New Testament. She was up to Luke and the miracles of Jesus, rejoicing in the miracle she'd seen herself.

"You're driving yourself too hard," Dane growled at her one evening when he stole her away. Grammy had agreed to spend the evening with Jeremy.

Robynn stared straight ahead, unwilling to spoil the evening with an argument. "Dane, you just don't understand."

"I understand all right. You need the money; that's what comes through loud and clear, or at least that's what you say."

"Look," she twisted in the seat so she could look him in the eye. "I'm not putting this kind of pressure on myself just for fun. I . . . Josh and I have a dream, and I'll do whatever it takes to get the cash I need." She laid a hand on his arm. "So please don't nag at me. It won't be for much longer."

Dane covered her hand with his own. "Princess Lady, we need to talk. Not just quick visits, but really talk."

She glanced at her watch. "I have to go in. Mother wants to get home, and as you so inelegantly put it, I look—"

"Beautiful," he interrupted her. "But that's not the last you'll hear from me." He climbed out of the car and came around her side to open the door. "I won't come in tonight. You need some rest." He took both her shoulders in his strong hands, then massaged his way up to her slender neck. When his thumbs brushed her parted lips, he bent his head and dusted each eye with his lips, nibbled the tip of her nose, and at last, found her mouth. His hands tangled in her hair as his breathing quickened. "Good night." He patted her on the shoulder as he turned her toward the house. Before Robynn had time to open the back door, the roar of his car's engine faded down the street.

Her mother met her at the door, coat in hand. "I'll see you in the morning, dear. Four forty-five as usual?"

"Yes." Robynn stopped her with a hand on her arm. "You could stay here, you know. We have a spare bedroom."

"I know, dear. But your father likes me home in bed with him."

"You could both stay here."

"See you later." The discussion was becoming a nightly thing.

"I'll never understand them if it takes a thousand years," Robynn muttered to herself as she shut off the lights.

With only the light from the hall, she tiptoed into Jeremy's room. He lay on his stomach, one arm wrapped around the koala bear, dark curls feathered across his forehead. The hollows were already filling in his cheeks, and the terrible pallor was disappearing. Each day his noise level seemed to rise another decibel. It was so good to have him home.

Her father came by the house at noon the next day to join them for lunch. The absence of his perennial smile triggered the worry in Robynn's mind before he even got his coat off.

"Okay, what is it?" She hung his coat in the closet.

"Hi, Grandpa." Jeremy ambled out of his room. "You gonna eat with us? Grammy fixed tuna sandwiches and chicken noodle soup. That's my favorite. Besides, hambuggers and hot dogs and..." He scrunched his face up, thinking hard.

Grandpa Ahern bent down to hug the little boy, then scooped him up in his arms.

Jeremy crowed with glee. Robynn laughed along, but inside, the worry gnawed at her.

With lunch over and Jeremy settled down with his talking books, she refused to be put off any longer. "All right." She refilled her father's coffee cup and sat down herself. "Let's have it."

"Well, I made a mistake with a couple of my investments and ... well

. . ." He took a deep breath. "I can't get my hands on the full amount I said I'd have for you."

Robynn stared at her hands. She heard the dreams shattering like falling glass. "How much?"

"How much can I invest?"

She nodded.

"Forty now. Twenty-five within a year, hopefully." He took a swallow of coffee. "I'm sorry, Princess. I did my best. I know that racing string is a good investment, but I'm borrowing as it is."

She stopped behind him to lay a hand on his shoulder. "Don't worry, Daddy. I'm not desperate—yet."

After the races that afternoon, Robynn called a real estate friend. "How soon could you sell my house?"

Silence weighted the line. "I'm sorry, Robynn, but right now isn't a good time to sell. Houses have been sitting on the market for months. We can hardly give them away."

Robynn groaned.

"I know. It's terrible. But what would you want to sell your house for, anyway? It's just perfect for you. Hey, this is me talking as your friend, not your favorite Realtor."

"I need the money."

"Good reason. Have you thought of a loan?"

"Yes. They gave me twenty-five thousand dollars. I need about a hundred and fifty." Robynn slumped down until she sprawled on the dusty blue carpet, her back against the wall.

"What about a personal loan at the bank?"

"For a hundred thousand? They talk in terms of ten without collateral. Remember, my house is now mortgaged to the hilt." Jeremy came and sat down between her legs. She dropped a kiss on the top of his head. "I gotta go. Thanks anyway." She reached up to replace the phone, then gave him a squeeze. "Oh, Jeremy, I love you, love you, love you." With the final "love you," she sneaked her fingers up to his rib cage and tickled.

Jeremy's head thumped her chest as he wriggled to get free. "No, Mommy," he giggled, squirming and twisting around. He stopped suddenly, tilting his head toward the front door. "Dane's here." He leaped to his feet. "Maybe he brought me some popsicles."

"Jeremy!" Robynn followed him, laughing in exasperation. "How many times have I warned you about asking for treats."

"I didn't." Jeremy turned, hands on hips. "He asked."

Dane became the hit of the evening when he invited them out for dinner. "Well, Tiger, where would you like to go?" "Don't ask him," Robynn said, pretend horror rounding her mouth.

"McDonald's," Jeremy stated as if there were no other place in the world, let alone Portland.

"I tried to warn you." Robynn laughed as she got their coats. "Maybe next time you'll listen to me."

When they got out of the car again, Jeremy walked in the middle, swinging both their hands like he'd grown up doing just that.

We look like any other American family out for dinner, Robynn thought as she caught their reflection in the swinging door. *Who's to know this is a first for us?* Her smile dimmed; too soon Jeremy would be going back to school. And Dane. What was it he wanted to talk to her about? Right now he probably wouldn't have any words left. He'd used them up on Jeremy.

"But why?" Jeremy asked for the umpteenth time.

"Why not?" Dane smiled down at him.

The scrunched-up look indicated Jeremy was thinking hard for a suitable reply.

"What do you want, Tiger?" Dane asked.

"A cheesebugger … umm … french fries and …"

"How about a chocolate shake?"

"Wow! Really? Mom never lets me have that."

Dane shrugged his shoulders apologetically, accompanied by a sheepish grin in Robynn's general direction.

"You're buying," is all she said.

"Mom wants Chicken McNuggets so I can have one," Jeremy stated. "And I like sweet and sour sauce."

"Hey, this is your mother's dinner. You already ordered yours."

"I know, but this is what we always order."

Robynn heard Dane mutter under his breath, "Lord protect us from small Caesars."

When they were seated at their table and Jeremy had said an extended grace, the conversation between Dane and Jeremy continued. Dane showed remarkable patience in answering all the questions. Robynn enjoyed it, watching both of them as she ate her dinner in peace. Usually she was the one on the answering end.

Then she began to feel left out. The two seemed to get along just great without her. *This is silly,* she scolded herself. *You want them to get to know each other; so don't interrupt. God, how come I can be so mixed up?*

By the last french fry, the question machine was wearing down, his drooping eyes testifying to his recent illness. Dane picked him up in one arm and with the other hand pulled Robynn to her feet. She was beginning to feel as drained as the child smiling over Dane's broad shoulder, one arm curled around the man's neck.

The ride home passed in silence. When Dane reached into the backseat to unbuckle Jeremy, the boy was sound asleep. Carefully he lifted the limp body out, no mean stunt in the cramped space of the low-slung car.

"We're going to need a bigger car," he grunted as he stood upright.

Robynn turned to him, startled.

"I warned you I'm a persistent man." Dane smiled back at her, his teeth flashing white in the dimness.

Robynn unlocked the back door and led the way to Jeremy's bedroom, flicking on the lights as she went.

Together they untied the knotted laces of the blue tennis shoes. Like a well-rehearsed team, they had Jeremy undressed and in bed without his ever waking. The sense of rightness persisted as they each kissed the small boy's cheek and Robynn tucked the bear in place in the crook of Jeremy's arm.

"Lord bless and keep you, my son," she whispered as she kissed his cheek again.

"Amen to that, and you, too." At the door Dane turned out the light and, leaving the door open a crack, followed Robynn into the living room.

"You're very good with him, you know." She smiled as she gestured toward the sofa. "Can you stay for a while?"

"No, I don't think I better." Dane suddenly seemed ill at ease.

Confusion creased Robynn's forehead. "What is it?"

"Robynn, loving you and leaving you, watching you ride, keeping myself under control when all I want to do is be with you and protect you—it's all driving me nuts. I can't sleep at night. A certain violet-eyed

Irishwoman keeps haunting my dreams. I can't stand it much longer." He clasped her in a bear hug, then nearly ran out the door.

His words echoed in her mind as she prepared for bed. The evening had been a perfect jewel until the gem cutter slipped and destroyed the facets. Her prayers that night centered on a certain stubborn Irishman.

Two days later a low-pressure bank still lay over Portland, bringing with it the ever-present drizzle. It would let up, then become showers. Robynn was never sure where one stopped and the other began. She didn't think the meteorologists on TV really knew either.

The track was soggy, and so were everyone's tempers. Even the horses were edgy, responding to the tension. Robynn's first mount for the morning workout, Finding Fun, lived up to her name. Halfway around the track she ploughed to a stop, then crow-hopped sideways, snorting at the fallen rider in front of them. Luckily for Robynn, she was prepared or she'd have landed in the soft sand like the inexperienced jockey picking himself up and brushing off the mud.

"You okay?" She pulled the prancing filly to a standstill.

"That worthless . . ." He carried on in his native Spanish as he slogged back across the infield.

"We have a new one to train," Dane said as she slipped off Finding Fun. "He's down in the end stall. Don't go near him by yourself. He looks to be a mean one."

"Josh won't take a mean animal, says they're too much trouble." They ambled companionably down the row of stalls.

A blood-red sorrel bared his teeth and lunged at them as they approached, his forefeet thundering his anger against the door.

Robynn stopped just beyond his reach and began her singsong, no particular words, just the crooning voice that worked wonders on animals and people alike.

This time was no different. The horse pointed his ears toward her, listening intently. The croon continued. The furious red hue left his eyes, he tossed his head one last time and stood at the door, inviting the light fingers she stroked down his nose. She rubbed his ears, his broad, flat cheekbones, and down the sweat-spotted neck. The horse blew in her hair and leaned into the stroking, his ears flicking back and forth at her singing.

Dane stood tense, ready to leap in to save her if necessary. "I can't believe what my own eyes see," he muttered as he watched them.

When she finally gave the horse one last pat and a piece of carrot from her ever-present supply, she turned to Dane. "Shall I get the next one out before this crummy weather becomes a downpour?"

"What are you, a horse whisperer or something?"

"No. Josh calls it my gift. For some reason I've always had a way with animals."

"Well, I wouldn't have believed it if I hadn't seen it." He turned her toward him as they reached the sanctuary of the tack room. "Maybe that's how you've captured me." Removing her helmet, he drew her into his arms and laid his cheek against her hair. "You scared me out of another night's sleep just now. What am I going to do with you?"

They both knew the question was rhetorical.

Each day the sorrel colt grew calmer, tolerating Dane, even in Robynn's absence. At first, two men worked the colt on ropes as a safety precaution. After several days they discarded the practice. The horse had already been broken to the track and starting gate before Josh had agreed to finish him out.

Getting Dane's permission was the hardest part of riding the frisky colt. The first morning out on the track, Dane rode the steady quarter horse they used for training, keeping a tight hold on the lead rope. The two-year-old Sunday Driver trotted along, head high, ears flicking to listen for Robynn's voice. He watched every horse on the track, whistled and snorted when one came near. She could feel his tension—poised and ready to react at any moment.

Robynn thrilled to the horse's display of barely leashed power. She watched his ears, alert to any change of mood, and grinned at Dane when she caught his gaze.

"Wow! This is some horse." She patted the sweaty shoulder and unbuckled the girth. "Whoever named him Sunday Driver sure made a mistake. He's more like a Fireball."

Dane's jaw tensed. Ignoring her banter, he cautioned, "You just be careful. Don't let up for a minute. He might like you but . . ."

The workout passed without incident and Robynn had a hard time keeping from saying "I told you so."

"You worry too much." Robynn slipped her arm through his, leaving the now docile Thoroughbred in his stall. "We'll have him ready for the geriatric set to ride within a week."

Robynn arrived at the track late the next morning. A traffic snarl had trapped her mother on the freeway. Daylight brightened the sky when she finally skidded into the lot, parked her car, and raced through the gate.

She dogtrotted down the row of stalls looking for Dane. As she ran, the high-pitched scream of an angry horse raised the hairs on the back of her neck.

The piercing whinny came again, this time with the answering challenge of another horse, lower pitched but just as furious.

Robynn dashed around the end of the barn and into the open area used to walk horses for the cool down.

Two men clung to the rope of a dark bay. They watched as the horse rose in the air, forelegs slashing at Sunday Driver. As the bay hit the ground, the men leaped to clamp their hands on his halter. Their combined weight forced his feet to stay on the ground.

Sunday Driver charged, teeth bared. But Dane, who had one hand on the halter, raised the other hand to strike the horse's nose. "Whoa!" At the force of his hand and commanding voice, the animal stopped and shook his head.

Dane's back had been turned to the other horse. Suddenly the bay reared again. A vicious forefoot dropped Dane to the ground like he'd been pole-axed.

When her stunned brain finally responded, Robynn rushed in to help. Every muscle and tendon quivered from the skirmish as Sunday Driver stood, head down, the lead rope caught beneath Dane's inert body.

Dane, Dane! her mind screamed, but she dared not take her eyes off the quivering horse until she had backed him away and handed the lead rope off to one of the waiting grooms.

By the time she moved back to Dane, two men were checking his pulse and eyes. Robynn knelt in the shavings by his head. His dark hair seemed even blacker in contrast to the pallor of his normally tan face.

"Dane, please be okay. Oh God, let him be all right." Her prayers to God and her entreaties to the fallen man intermingled, along with tears that flowed unheeded down her cheeks.

"I've called the ambulance," a man behind her said.

Robynn nodded, vaguely aware of who spoke. Tenderly, she explored the back of Dane's head with her fingertips. As her fingers caressed his scalp, she felt hair matted and moist. Her hand came away streaked with blood.

"He's bleeding! Someone get a bandanna quick." Robynn reached up and within seconds had been handed a makeshift bandage for Dane's wound. She remembered her first aid training—apply pressure. She gently placed the dressing over the bleeding area and held it tightly against his head.

He could be dying, and you never even told him you love him, a voice from her mind jeered. *You might not get the chance now.*

But he can't die. We have too much living to do—together. Together . . .

"Dane," she whispered, "you'll be all right. Remember that. You can't leave your family."

The red and white ambulance pulled up beside them. Two men scrambled out and within moments had a stretcher on the ground, ready for the injured man.

As they lifted him onto the canvas cot, Dane's eyelids fluttered open. "Wha . . . what hit me?" he muttered, trying to raise his hand to his head. He couldn't.

"That crazy bay." Robynn had been holding both his hands in a vicelike grip. Now, under his scrutiny, she slowly released her hold.

Dane sat up. "Easy now," the attendant said. "You've had a nasty crack on the head." He probed the area gently.

"Ouch!" Dane flinched. "How's that fool, Sunday Driver?"

At the disgruntled tone in his voice, laughter from sheer joy got the better of her. She tried to stifle the sound, but Dane heard her.

"What's so funny? I nearly get my head kicked off and you stand there laughing." A smile lurked in the blue of his eyes, but he grimaced when he turned his head too quickly. He stood, leaning his weight on her.

"You'll probably need X-rays," the attendant suggested. "You never know about head injuries."

"Thanks anyway, but I'll take a rain check on the ambulance. Leave the ride for those who really need it. Little Merry Sunshine here can take care of me."

"Dane Morgan! You sit down and let them take a look at that wound." Her eyes flashed up at him. "You may need stitches if nothing else." Surprised at the command in her voice, he obeyed.

"It's just a scalp wound, although you'll have quite a goose egg back there." The attendant cleansed the wound expertly as he gave them instructions. "If you have continuing headaches, blurred vision, or vomiting, you'd better get yourself to emergency pronto."

"He will," Robynn assured them as they replaced their equipment. By now, seeing Dane was safe, everyone else had gone back to work.

"Well, look who's giving the orders now." He stood again, letting Robynn take some of his weight, as they shuffled back to the tack room.

"Somebody has to have some sense around here."

Dane chuckled carefully, trying not to move his head.

"Does it hurt terribly?" She looked up to catch the glinting amusement. "What are you laughing at?"

"You, Princess. Just listen to yourself. You order me to take it easy when you've been driving yourself to the point of exhaustion for weeks. And you're the one with sense?"

Robynn grinned sheepishly. "But Dane, you scared me to death back there. Those horses out of control, you lying unconscious on the ground."

"To quote a very bright person I know, 'Accidents can happen just as easily on the freeway as on the track.'" He lowered himself into one of the chairs. "Ah-h-h. That's better."

Ahem, Robynn, her internal voice counseled. *Now you know how he's been feeling all this time. It tears you up inside when someone you love is hurt. You knew that for Jeremy. Now admit it for Dane. You love him. Tell him so.*

Her mind played with the words. *I love you, Dane Morgan. Dane, I love you, love you, love you . . .*

"Dane, I . . ." She placed a hand on his shoulder and started again. "I . . ."

One of the grooms stuck his head through the doorway. "How's he doing?"

Dane nodded without opening his eyes, "Fine."

"Good. Josh said to call him as soon as you could. He phoned a few minutes ago."

"News sure travels fast around here." Dane rose from his chair. "Let's go get a cup of coffee and call him from there. Then we've got to get to work. We're running way behind."

The moment for declaring love had passed. *I'll tell him later,* Robynn promised herself. Later didn't come. Pressures of daily work increased as time flew by. The racing program had ended before they could find a moment together.

"I'll feed the horses for you tonight." She pushed him out the door after they returned to the barns. "You go home and get some sleep. You'll feel better in the morning."

"Yes, Mother Hen." A drawn smile revealed his exhaustion. "John Simms will be over in a few minutes. He asked if he could help, and I took him up on it. See you in the morning."

"Tomorrow," she promised Finding Fun as she poured grain in the filly's manger. "I'll tell him tomorrow."

TEN

When she arrived back at the track after her break the next afternoon, Robynn parked the Celica and went directly to the jockeys' dressing rooms. The first race of the day was already under way, showing on the monitor screen. It looked like a mud bath. Halfway around the track, and it was almost impossible to tell who was who. When the straining horses crossed the wire, Robynn breathed a sigh of relief.

No accidents.

"Bet there's a lot of hot legs from that race." She hung her silks on the hooks above the benches. "Probably lamed half the horses out there."

By the time she stepped on the scales with all her gear in hand, Robynn felt more jittery than normal. She hated a muddy track even worse than Jim Dandy did. All the slipping and sliding. She'd had her worst fall on a day just like today. A dislocated shoulder and two cracked ribs laid her up for over a week. Sheer guts beat the pain for weeks after that.

Don't look back, she reminded herself. *Think up. Today is gonna be a great day. You've got races to win and the horses that can do it. You're a good rider with a good mind. You know you can do it.* After the pep talk, she took a deep breath and shrugged her shoulders up tight to her ears and lowered them again to relax the tense muscles.

"You okay, Princess?" John Simms waited beside her for the horses to be led into the saddling paddock.

"Sure." She put on a smile, just for his benefit, then added some life to her second. "Sure. Of course. It's a great day."

"Yeah, just marvelous if your feet are webbed and you quack instead of whinny or talk."

"Why, John, you sound downright anti-Oregon. I thought everyone developed webbed feet after awhile. I'll show you mine sometime."

"F-u-n-n-y. But if you're showing off, it isn't your webbed feet I'd like to see."

"John!"

He tried to leer at her, but the sight of her scandalized face sent his crow of delight bouncing off the murky ceiling beams.

The blush that stained her cheeks stayed with her as she circled the stalls to find her mount. Dane and Jim Dandy waited on the far side.

"Who's been teasing you now?" He lifted the saddle from her arms and positioned it just behind the horse's withers.

"Oh, that John . . ."

"He's sure up on a mean one over there." Dane nodded over his shoulder. "That black tried to kick Dandy here as we came in."

Robynn stole a glance at the man giving her a leg up. His jaw looked clamped as a sprung bear trap, his fine lips thinned to a narrow line. When his eyes met hers, the steel of suppressed fury bolted through her like a stray lightning shaft.

Robynn shivered.

She tore her gaze from the ice blue one and concentrated on what he was saying. The shivers running up and down her back had nothing to do with the weather.

Here we go again, back to the old yo-yo. Maybe I'm the yo-yo after all. Thoughts chased each other through her brain like frisking colts on a brisk fall morning.

"You know what to do as well as anyone," Dane continued. "There're only five entered, but watch out for that black. If you can get out in front, so much the better. You know how Dandy hates mud in his face."

Robynn stroked down the satiny neck and reached forward to scratch right behind the horse's ears. "We'll be fine," she crooned as much to settle herself as the colt and the man beside her. "Not to worry."

As they walked from the dimness of the paddock into the falling mist, her horse fell into step alongside the pony rider. Jim Dandy reached out in a smooth, flat-footed walk, his ears pricked, anticipation evident in every rippling muscle.

By the time they reached the starting gates, Robynn had put Dane out of her mind. All her concentration zeroed in on Jim Dandy and the race at hand.

The horses were nearly in the gate when the black snorted in fury, slashed at the handler, and reared straight in the air. Robynn caught a glimpse of Simms clinging like a burr on the furious animal. When the black came down again, John turned him and walked him around in a tight circle.

"Easy, fella," Robynn sang her song of calm. "You don't have to pay any attention to him. He's just a troublemaker." Jim Dandy danced a moment with his front feet, then settled back on his haunches as the gate closed behind the fussing horse.

With her goggles in place, Robynn sucked in a deep lung full of air, let it out in a whoosh to relax, and tangled her fingers in a hunk of mane. The gates clanged open. Dandy leaped forward. As he found his stride, Robynn felt him slip. She tightened the reins, feeling the uncertainty in his mouth. When he felt secure again, the pack was already in front of them, pounding hooves showering everything with sloppy mud. A crack opened between the two in front, and Robynn urged Dandy forward. Straight and true, he drove up the middle, his ears flat against his head.

As Robynn debated whether to swing around on the outside of the next two in front of her, the black slipped. In that split second, he careened against his running mate, and before anyone had time to change course, both animals and jockeys became a mass of flailing legs and thrashing bodies. No one knew whether the screams were from the horses or jockeys. Even as Robynn felt Dandy gather himself, he leaped into the air and over the fallen entries. He slipped as his feet hit the mud again, but Robynn kept the reins taut, helping him stay upright. The delayed-action panic grabbed her guts.

As they passed under the wire, Robynn heard herself crying, "Dear God, make them be all right. Please! Please!" As she slowed Jim Dandy and turned toward the winner's circle, she could see the ambulance attendants picking up both riders. One horse, head hanging down, leaned against the rail, taking the pressure off a front leg. The black was still down.

At the winner's circle, Robynn slipped from her horse's back and quickly unbuckled the saddle girth. One look at Dane's bloodless face, and she felt the fear grab her insides again. For just a moment she leaned against her mud-caked horse, waiting for the weakness to leave her knees so she could walk.

"Congratulations, O'Dell." The race master laid the horseshoe of red and white roses over Jim Dandy's withers. "That was quick thinking out there."

"Not on my part." Robynn stroked her horse's muddy neck. "It was all Jim Dandy here. I just hung on."

Robynn's smile for the cameras never made it past the twitch of her mouth. She stopped one of the owners she knew.

"How bad?"

"John's unconscious, bleeding from a head wound."

"Oh, no..."

"It's ribs and a leg for the other. The black broke his neck." He shook her gloved hand. "Congratulations on your quick thinking out there. It could have been worse."

Robynn forced herself not to look back at the track where the accident had happened, but her mind knew about the truck and winch that came to pick up the dead animal. There would be extra time between the two races to clean up the mess and drag the track again.

She staggered as she stepped onto the scale. The scale master's strong hand caught her and held her upright until she regained her balance.

"Thanks," she muttered past the tears clogging her throat. She wasn't sure if they were for John, the horses, or relief that she was still in one piece. Shivers attacked her again, so strong the scale refused to balance. Robynn breathed deeply, forcing herself to stand still. At the master's nod, she stepped down and slammed into a tall, rock solid chest. Dane wrapped both arms around her, saddle and all. Robynn shivered again as his warmth penetrated her frozen bones.

"Come on, you little idiot." He took the saddle from her clenched arms. "Let's get you out of the rain." With one strong arm around her, Dane almost carried her into the shelter of the stands.

Robynn took off her helmet and, shaking out her hair, leaned against him, grateful for both his warmth and caring. She could hear his heart thundering beneath her ear. How nice it felt to be held, leaving other arms to fight off the rain and cold for her.

"Hurry and get showered and I'll take you home," Dane murmured against her hair.

"Home?" Robynn stared up at him. "But I've got three other races to run."

"After what happened out there?"

"What do you mean?" Robynn shook her head as the steel-trap jaw closed above her. "That was an accident."

"You stubborn woman." The shake he administered was not gentle. "You could have been killed out there, like that black beast."

"But I wasn't."

"No, not this time. And not any time if I have anything to say about it."

Robynn borrowed the steel from his jaw to stiffen her spine. "But you don't have anything to say about it." She stepped back, chin tilted, nostrils flaring, her princess mask back in place. "I *am* a jockey. Racing horses is my job. And accident or no, I do my job."

The force of the saddle being dumped into her arms sent Robynn reeling back against the concrete wall. The fury in his eyes impaled her in place.

When her breath returned, Robynn turned and stumbled into the dressing rooms. "Blast him," she muttered. "When is he going to quit worrying about me?" With great skill, she ignored the voice that reminded her how she had felt when Dane was struck down—and what he'd said about his mother.

"He has an overdeveloped sense of responsibility, that's all. He'll just have to get over it." She could feel her steam of anger dissipate as she muttered.

ELEVEN

The more Robynn thought about Dane's behavior, the angrier she became. Of all the high-handed—hollering at her like that with other people around—and on top of that, her head ached where she had banged it against the concrete. He'd almost thrown the saddle at her.

"Well, if that's the way he wants it, that's the way he'll have it." She glared at her reflection in the mirror. Her violet eyes sparked darts, daggers, and a promise to get even.

Each time she settled in the saddle on another horse, she pulled her mind back from the earlier disaster and tried to concentrate on the race at hand. It wasn't easy.

Reports came back from the hospital. John would be all right. The concussion was of medium severity. Having experienced a mild one herself, Robynn knew he felt like retiring from the land of feeling for a time.

The jockeys congregated by the scale in their spare moments to discuss the accident.

"He'll feel more like having visitors tomorrow," Robynn reminded them. "At least the hospital's put both jockeys in the same room. Even on the same floor as Josh. They must have had us in mind, trying to make visiting easy."

"Yeah," Pam replied. "That hospital is gonna get 'em well real fast, before they drive the nurses totally nuts."

By the last race of the day, Robynn still had not seen Dane. He'd sent the horses over by a groom. Each time, her anger boiled a little closer to the surface. Her final mount was the cantankerous gray he had warned her about. Robynn drove the animal under the wire, ahead by a length, just to spite him.

Robynn smiled amid the congratulations for a day of superior riding. The stands buzzed with the way she and Jim Dandy had avoided the fall.

However, none of the smiles, handshakes, and good wishes meant anything without Dane's special smile, his hug, his words of praise.

Anger turned to disappointment as she turned out of the locker room to face an empty wall. Somehow, she'd hoped he'd be there. The wall wasn't the only thing that needed to be held up right now.

"Pull yourself together," she ordered as she climbed into her car. "You can't go home to Jeremy looking like this. He's too sensitive to your moods."

"Jeremy's been a handful today!" Grammy said as she met her daughter at the door. "I finally had to send him to his room."

"I'm sorry, Mom." Robynn gave her a big hug. "Maybe the weather is affecting him, too."

"Well, something certainly is." Grammy went out the door, shaking her head.

"Bad day, huh, Tiger?" Robynn asked as she turned on the light in his bedroom. She sat down on the edge of his bed. Jeremy buried his head in her lap. "Grammy's mad at me."

His lower lip stuck out far enough to rest his koala bear on it.

"What did you do?"

"Nothing."

"What were you supposed to do?" She stroked the curling hair back from his forehead. *It's amazing,* she thought, *how much he resembles Dane. Same black, curly hair. Same blue eyes. Whoa, girl,* she commanded herself. *You're mad at that man, remember?*

"I didn't want soup for lunch. I want hot dogs."

"But we're out of hot dogs. You ate them yesterday."

The stubborn thrust of his lip revealed his state of mind. "And I asked for a popsicle."

"We're out of those, too. Tomorrow is grocery day."

"Grammy didn't want to take me to the store."

"I should guess not. You've been a pill, but . . ." Robynn wrapped both arms around him and squeezed. "I love you, anyway. And so does Grammy." She leaned over and planted a smacking kiss on his ear.

Jeremy scrubbed it off with one fist, but smiles returned to his mouth. A giggle escaped when she blew on his scrunched, closed eyelids. "When's Dane coming?" He sat up as if expecting to hear the car any moment.

"Probably not tonight." Robynn chewed her lip. "I–I think he had something else planned."

"Does he still have a bump on his head?"

"Yes."

"Maybe he has a headache. He better go to bed." Jeremy delivered his medical pronouncement with all the seriousness of a practicing physician.

"You tell him, Tiger." She took his hand, and together they walked out to the living room. "Want some pop? I'm going to have some."

Robynn read two complete books to Jeremy before he finally fell asleep. The phone hadn't rung. No silver Porsche roared up the street.

Even though she thought of calling Dane, she phoned Josh instead, hoping he might mention Dane. They talked of the day's racing, the accident, the amount of money they were short—but not about Dane.

Robynn went to bed, self-pity bickering with righteous anger. "Jesus," she prayed. "It's hard to be thankful when you're mad at someone, but I sure appreciate the way You kept everyone alive today—and yesterday." She sighed before going on. "Thank You for keeping me safe today. Can't Dane see what a miracle that was and be glad with me? What is he, a pouter? Why just yesterday everything was fine again. I hate feeling jerked around."

She thumped her pillow. "So . . . I praise You for giving my horse wings today and for sending Your Son to die for me, and for loving me when, like right now, I don't feel very lovable. God, I need a hug, a Dane hug." She smiled in the darkness. "And I bet he does, too. Yesterday . . ."

Yesterday. Her thoughts roamed. *Yesterday I almost told Dane how much I care for him.*

"Yes-ter-day . . ." The old song hummed through her mind, lulling her to sleep.

Robynn woke in the morning with a different song on her mind. This was a child's song, a Bible verse set to music. "Be kind to one another, forgiving one another even as God in Christ has forgiven you." The catchy tune ran over and over as she pulled on worn jeans and a red wool sweater over her turtleneck. The song persisted as she waved good-bye to her mother. The hum of windshield wipers refused to drown out the words.

"All right!" She laughed at her reflection in the rearview mirror. "I get the message." She still whistled the tune as she skipped down the stalls, searching for the man she loved.

Ed Bannon, a longtime friend of Josh's, was feeding the horses and reading instructions from a list in his hand.

"Hey, Ed. Where's Dane?" Robynn asked, a small knot of worry tightening under her ribs.

"I don't know. All's I know is Josh called me last night and asked me to take care of the horses 'til he gets back. Said you'd know about the training and racing. I'm to get more instructions this morning when I see him after chores is done."

Robynn collapsed on the box in the tack room. She felt like she'd been thrown from a horse and all the wind knocked out of her. *He's gone. I know it. Dane's gone.*

"I'll be back in a bit," she called as she leaped to her feet. She ran back out the gate and flung her car door open. *He can't be gone, she reasoned. He must be at Josh's apartment. Somehow we've got to talk.*

The hope buoyed her until she pulled into the cul-de-sac. There were no lights and no silver Porsche. Only Josh's tired old pickup waited in the driveway. Biting her lip, she got out of the car and rang the doorbell. Finally, she leaned against the bell, willing, praying, for Dane to answer.

Nothing.

Nothing was the color of the morning as she finished her duties so she could visit Josh. She was a jockey, she reminded herself when she wanted to run away and cry. And with a jockey, the horses came first. Horses deserved more than desertion.

"I'll never be understanding it myself, Princess." The lines on Josh's face had deepened overnight. "He came in here last night like a house afire. Said on top of what was going on here, he had an emergency back in San Francisco. Ed agreed to take over." Josh slammed his fist into the mattress. "If I don't get out of here pretty soon, everything'll be shot beyond redemption."

"We'll get along, Josh." Robynn raised her chin. "You just get better. I've managed a long time without our so-called friend. I'll manage again." Shoulders back, she marched out the door.

From the smiling princess mask secured on Robynn's face in the following days, no one knew what the tears were doing to her inside. "He had an emergency," she responded when questioned about Dane. Finally, Pam cornered her before she could slip out the door.

"Okay," Pam demanded as they walked out to the parking lot after the final race. "What gives with you? Did you send him packing or what?"

Robynn repeated her canned speech, "Mr. Morgan . . ."

"Stow it, Princess. This is Pam. You know, your old friend Pam. The one who can see beyond that mask of yours." She stopped abruptly at the sight of the mirrored pain in Robynn's eyes. "I'll kill him," Pam muttered. "I swear, I'll kill that man. Anyone who would hurt you like that deserves to be shot."

Robynn took a deep breath. It took all the force in her lungs to get enough air past the huge lump that had taken up permanent residence in her chest.

"Thanks for your concern, lady." She tossed the duffel bag in the backseat of the Celica. "You're a good friend."

"Go to dinner with me. Maybe talking will make you feel better."

"Thanks. But tomorrow Jeremy goes back to school, so I need to get his stuff together. Maybe another time."

Jeremy had stopped asking about Dane. But Robynn noticed that he stopped whatever he was doing to listen intently whenever a sports car roared by. Each time, the sound faded away completely before he went back to what he was doing. "Hurry Jeremy, or we'll be late for church."

"I don't want to go. I want Dane to come. You call him, okay?"

"Sorry, Tiger, I don't know his phone number."

"You could call information."

"You're right. I'll think about it, okay? You go wash your face, and we'll be outa here. I bet we could find a hot fudge sundae on the way home."

"Yeah." Two minutes later they were out the door.

As usual, the singing lifted her spirits and the sermon seemed written just for her. God promised again to never leave nor forsake her.

Not like some men I know, she thought before forcing her mind to concentrate on the verses being read.

Back home, after all Jeremy's clothes were packed, Robynn and her son cuddled on the sofa in front of the fireplace. If she just closed her eyes, she could see Dane lying there on the rug.

"Mommy, keep reading." Jeremy tugged at her arm.

She finished the story and closed the book. "Time for bed, Son. Go brush your teeth and I'll be right in. Oh, and make sure you get all the fudge off." Jeremy ran off, giggling.

Robynn closed her eyes again. She could feel the play of Dane's muscles as she leaned against his broad chest, smell the tang of his aftershave.

"Mom!" The tone was demanding, like this wasn't the first time Jeremy had called.

The next morning, Robynn pasted her princess smile back in place and forcefully injected cheer into her voice as she and Jeremy left for school. To pass time on the drive down the Willamette Valley, she told him stories: David, the giant killer, and Samuel, a boy called by God. Jeremy's favorite was Moses.

"Let my people go," he chanted with her when they came to the part about Moses and Pharaoh. "Let my people go."

Mrs. C welcomed him back with a big hug and dishes of chocolate ice cream for the children in his cottage. Robynn kissed him good-bye and left him, the star bragging about his stay in the hospital.

She tried to brighten up for Josh the next day. His good news? He'd be graduating to crutches by the end of the week. Finally he would be able to leave the hospital.

But each of the lonely nights back at her house, she alternated between anger and hurt, worry and fear. Was Jeremy really all right at school? Where in the world was Dane? Why didn't he at least call? That always brought her back to anger, and the cycle continued.

Until she gave up and prayed it all out again.

"You must get tired of me saying the same thing every night." She swallowed the tears again and opened her Bible, searching for the promises God meant just for her. Psalm 91 helped. The thought of being safe under the pinions of His mighty wings made it possible to sleep.

She perked up a couple nights later at the hospital when Josh handed her a letter from Opal. She had accepted their new offer of half the money down and the rest within a year. The racing string was theirs. "That's great, Josh. When you get out of here, we can look for some good pastureland."

"Aye." His eyes grew dreamy. "And maybe I'll be findin' a farm I can afford. Ten acres with a wee house."

She gave him a hug. "You will."

Each evening when she returned to her house, the emptiness struck her anew. Empty. What a dismal word. One Wednesday evening she dialed the area code for Pasadena and asked for the Dane Morgan residence.

"I'm sorry, ma'am, but that is an unlisted number." She felt like slamming the phone down but set it back gently. *Tomorrow,* she promised herself, *tomorrow I ask Josh.*

At church that evening, the pastor warned about self-pity. "When you're feeling low," he said, "look up. Look to the Christ who bears our burdens. Look to His hands, nailed for our sins. Look up. Look out. There's someone who needs you."

Robynn shook his hand at the door. "Thank you," she said. "I needed that."

For the first time in days, a smile curved her lips as she fell asleep. She'd made the decision: no more yo-yo. After the races on Sunday, she would fly to San Francisco and find Dane. Josh surely must have his address. After all, they were related.

And if he didn't? She'd call every construction company in town if she had to. How hard would it be to find a construction company called Morgan something or other? This time, *she* was going to do some talking and *he* was going to do some listening. And if he still insisted on marriage *or* racing? Well, so be it. They'd cross that bridge when they came to it. If he thought he was going to run out on her, he had another think coming. She refused to allow herself to think negative thoughts. As the pastor said, "Look up."

Sunday dawned with the sun streaking gold and vermilion on scattered clouds and painting Mount Hood the rarest of pinks. When Robynn breathed deeply the crisp, stinging air, she coughed. The boulder in her throat was gone. Someone had rolled it away during the night.

As if celebrating what might be the last sunny day of the racing season, the stands filled early. The Pacific Futura, a race for maiden colts, had drawn a lot of publicity. Sunday Driver was Robynn's mount. She found it hard to believe this was the same colt who had precipitated Dane's accident.

The fiery animal broke from the gate straight and true and never looked at another horse as he leveled out, driving hard for the finish, ahead by a length.

It was a good way to start the day's program.

The day continued with Robynn in the money in every race. The tension built toward the finale, the Race for the Roses, Portland's prestigious sweepstakes. Robynn had never won this race before. Neither had Sonny.

When Ed Bannon brought Finding Fun up to the saddling paddock, Robynn felt a thrill of anticipation. The two of them were already linked as winners.

She rubbed Finding's nose and up behind her ears. With a sigh, the filly leaned into her chest, begging for more. Robynn pushed her away. "You're getting hair all over me," she laughed. Ed boosted her into the saddle. As Robynn leaned over to adjust the stirrup, she felt a tingle up her spine.

Startled, she straightened and carefully searched the sea of faces surrounding the fence. Nothing.

"Well, girl, this is it," Robynn crooned as the filly stretched out in her ground-eating walk. When they entered the starting gate, she pulled her goggles into place and wrapped one hand in a hank of mane.

"The flag is up!" The announcer blared as at the clang of the gates, eleven horses catapulted into action. The crowds screamed for their favorites. All Robynn heard was the grunting and blowing of the straining horses. Steadily, stride by stride, Finding Fun and a bay pulled out of the pack. At the far turn, Robynn made her bid.

"Go, Finding," she yelled into her flickering ears. The bay on the rail beside them reacted at the same time.

Nose for nose, they thundered for the wire. At the last moment, Robynn tapped the sorrel's shoulder with the bat. Finding Fun leaped forward, winner by a head.

Robynn stood high in her stirrups, the thrill of victory welling like a geyser bursting from the ground. She laughed aloud. They had done it. They'd won the Race for the Roses.

Back in the winner's circle, Robynn and Finding Fun received thundering ovations. Robynn grinned and waved, feeling like the Queen of England facing her subjects.

When she slipped from the filly's back and unbuckled the girth, she again felt that familiar tingle start at her toes and race for the top of her helmet.

As the coveted horseshoe of red roses was draped over Finding's withers, Portland's mayor stepped forward. She placed a dozen long-stemmed red roses in Robynn's arms and kissed her on both cheeks.

The tingle sprinted up her spine again.

When the mayor took her arm and presented her to the roaring crowd, she saw him.

The tall, broad-shouldered man in a sheepskin jacket filled her range of vision. In his arms he carried a small, curly headed boy with hair the color of a raven's wing, just like the man's. The two looked so alike they could be father and son.

She barely noticed the old man, leaning on crutches at their side.

It could be said she hardly noticed anything. She couldn't tear her eyes away from the shocking blue gaze of the man staring with equal intensity at her. Ideas hummed along that gaze—dreams, apologies, and forgiveness asked and received.

The crowd parted like the Red Sea, leaving her an open aisle. Robynn O'Dell, the Princess, walked it proudly, cradling the roses in her arms. Their gazes never faltered.

Dane opened his other arm and Robynn walked into the curve of it, the roses clutched in her left hand. It left the right one free to hug both the man and the little boy.

"Mommy," Jeremy's voice rang out clearly. "Dane's gonna be my new daddy and we're gonna live on Opal's farm."

Robynn's look questioned Dane, then flicked to Josh. She smiled up at Jeremy. "We'll see, Son."

"And right the laddie is." Josh beamed, a tiny bit of moisture filming his eyes. "Dane here bought out the man who bought her out." The older man studied Robynn's face for a long moment, as if searching for her response, then shook his head. "Hey Tiger, how about grabbing on to my crutch here and we'll see about some ice cream." Dane set the boy down, never taking his eyes from Robynn's.

"You're finished here for the day?"

"Yes."

"Good, then we have some talking to do."

"Hey, Princess, you got some words for the press?"

"Be right there." She sent a questioning glance Dane's way.

"You go ahead. I'll be waiting right here."

She almost asked, "You sure you won't leave?" but smiled instead. "I'll hurry."

After answering questions for both print and television, she turned to the last man.

"So, did I hear right? There are wedding bells in the offing?"

Robynn could feel a blush work its way up her neck and over her cheeks. "I . . . we . . ." She glanced over at Dane, who lounged against the fence. He nodded and touched a finger to his forehead.

"No comment right now, Dave. Catch me later." Robynn made her way back to where Dane waited, stopping only to sign a couple programs thrust her way.

"Who's taking care of the horses?"

"Ed is, with Josh there to boss him. Your folks took Jeremy home with them. How soon can you get changed?" He held her elbow in a firm but gentle grip, walking so fast she had to dogtrot to keep up.

"Dane. Slow down."

"Oh, sorry." He gave her a sheepish smile and at least let her feet touch the ground every few feet.

Pam hummed a few bars of "Here Comes the Bride," when Robynn darted into the dressing room. "Hear ye! Clear the way. Our princess is in a royal hurry to meet her prince."

"Pam, knock it off."

"So, when's the date?"

"I haven't said yes yet." Robynn pulled up her jeans and snapped them, grabbing a clean shirt and sweater without even a minute's pause.

"So . . . are you?"

"He's got some explaining to do." Robynn stuffed her dirty things in the duffel, then grinned at her friend. "And then I'll hog-tie him so he can't leave again." She shoved her arms in the sleeves of her leather jacket and was out the door before the women quit laughing.

Once in the car, a four-wheel-drive SUV this time, Dane started the ignition and then asked, "Are you hungry, thirsty, or . . . ?"

"Or."

"Or?"

"I've got questions, you've got answers. You've got questions, I've got answers. So start." She snapped her seat belt and settled against the leather seat.

Dane stared straight ahead, wrists draped over the steering wheel. "Me first, huh?"

"Yep." Robynn could feel her heart pounding. Surely he didn't have some deep dark secret that would prevent their life together.

"Okay." He shifted into drive and joined the line of cars leaving the parking lot. "Remember when I told you how back when I was a little kid my father left for another tour of duty in the Marine Corps and made me promise to look after my mother and my sister?"

Robynn nodded. "In the chapel at the hospital."

"I took the charge seriously, so when my mother was permanently paralyzed in a steeplechase accident, I figured it was my fault. I had let my father, who returned from duty in a casket, down. I failed. I promised myself I would never let the woman I fell in love with be injured."

"Oh, Dane, I . . . I kinda figured as much."

He held up a hand. "Let me finish while I can. My mother raked me over the coals for my overbearing attitude many times, especially when I told her about you. I won't tell you what my sister said, but rest assured, they are both on your side. So I have had to do some deep thinking, and the emergency in my company was a good excuse to beat a hasty and totally ungentlemanly retreat. My mother's words."

He took the Highway 14 exit after crossing the I-5 bridge going north. "Your turn. Why didn't you tell me earlier about Jeremy?"

"I didn't want him hurt in case you decided to leave."

Dane flinched. "And I left."

She nodded.

"And he got hurt ?"

Another nod.

"Will you forgive me?"

"Yes, and we both already have. I finally had to make a commitment, or recommitment if you will, to my faith in Jesus. I got sick and tired of yo-yoing back and forth. I want God at the center of my life from now on, and any relationship we have has to be based on that principle."

"I have no problem with that." He took the turnoff to Orchards.

"Where are we going?"

"You'll see. I grew up in the church like you did and, like you, let other things get in the way. Jeremy's illness was the take-it-or-leave-it point. I just mess things up without Jesus Christ as my center. And you got hurt because of it. Another thing to forgive me for."

"Done." Robynn leaned her head back against the seat and turned to watch Dane's face. "So, anything else to reveal? I am looking forward to meeting your mother and sister, by the way. I've never had a sister before."

Dane covered her hand with his. "They'll love you, but not nearly as much as I do."

The simple statement made her eyes burn. "Ah, Dane."

They turned into the drive for McKecknen Stables and parked by the pasture of young stock. Halfway out of the car, Dane leaned back to ask, "Are you coming?"

"Okay." But before she could unbuckle her seat belt, he was around to open her car door. He took her hand and waved the other in an arc to encompass the farm.

"What do you think?"

"Of what?" She gave him a puzzled look.

"Of our farm."

"You really did buy it?"

"Lock, stock, and horseflesh."

"So Jeremy wasn't just confused?" Robynn leaned against the fence. The three yearlings trotted up to nose her sleeve and beg for treats.

"Not at all, but I have one more question." He dug in his pocket and pulled out a gray ring box.

Robynn turned her back to the horses so she could watch his face.

"Robynn O'Dell, will you marry me and be the Princess of all this?"

She now understood what people meant when they said her heart stopped.

"Dane, I–I want to keep racing." There, it was out. Her heart took up an unknown rhythm.

"Okay, but how about if only on our own horses? Not racing for other stables. Would that be a fair compromise?" He paused. "You can see I've given this a lot of thought."

Robynn closed her eyes. Her *Thank You, heavenly Father* winged heavenward before she lifted her eyes to see Dane studying her. While he'd leaned one arm on the white board fence so his hand almost touched her shoulder, his face said he was anything but relaxed.

"Of course I'll marry you." She raised her face for his long overdue kiss.

"Um, one thing."

"What?" She leaned back in his arms to study his face.

"You haven't said if you love me yet."

"Oh, I do, Dane Morgan. I love you now and for always." This time she kissed him.

"Ouch." He drew back and glared at the three colts. The middle one nodded as if he'd just done something of major importance. Dane rubbed his shoulder.

"Shame on you, Rowdy. You are not to bite." Robynn looked up at her husband-to-be. "You want me to kiss it and make it better?"

Dane growled, and both hands at her waist, swung her up in a circle. "Those three better get ready to race for their own roses because we've already won ours." He kissed her again, this time leaving her breathless. "I take it you want roses in our wedding?"

"Of course, but it's a good thing there are plenty of hothouse ones year around because I'm not waiting until June."

"How about red ones for Christmas?"

Robynn nodded. "I always was partial to long-stemmed red roses or else ones braided into a blanket or horseshoe." She snuggled against his chest. "Tell me I'm not dreaming."

"You are definitely not dreaming, Mrs.-Dane-Morgan-to-be. Or else we are in the same dream together." They stepped away from the fence just as the colt stuck out his nose for another warning. "Dreams full of love and roses."

ABOUT THE AUTHOR

*L*auraine Snelling is the bestselling author of over seventy books, both fiction and nonfiction, historical and contemporary, for adults and young readers. Lauraine and her husband Wayne live in California with a Basset Hound named Winston. To learn more about the author, you can visit www.laurainesnelling.com.